SAM AND ANGIE

SAM AND ANGIE

a novel by
Margaret Sweatman

TURNSTONE PRESS

Turnstone Press gratefully acknowledges the assistance of
the Canada Council and the Manitoba Arts Council.

This is a work of fiction. The characters described are fictitious,
as are the events of the story. Any resemblance to persons
living or dead is purely coincidental.

Excerpts from this novel have appeared in slightly altered
form in *Books in Canada,* and in *Prairie Fire.*

Front cover photograph: Debra Mosher

Design: Manuela Dias

This book was printed and bound in Canada
by Friesens for Turnstone Press.

Canadian Cataloguing in Publication Data

Sweatman, Margaret

Sam and Angie

ISBN 0-88801-208-X

I. Title.

PS8587.W36S3 1996   C813'.54   C96-920095-1
PR9199.3.S936S3 1996

Contents

ACKNOWLEDGEMENTS

The writer is very grateful to the Manitoba Arts Council, Canada Council, and the Ontario Arts Council for their support during the composition of this book.

And to Glenn Buhr, Barbara Schott, Charlene Diehl-Jones, David Arnason, Lindy Clubb, Bill Arbuthnot (key grip), Scott Sweatman, Linda Ostry, Turnstone Press, Lorraine Sweatman, Alan Sweatman, and my daughters Bailey Harris and Hillery Harris, love and gratitude.

PART ONE

Dancing in the Dark

On that June night when the rain finally broke the drought, Sam's house was devoted to homesick violins and a gospel choir. Rain blended magically with percussive horns, the slide and shine of the snare, warm waltz rhythms of a double bass, and the smooth-throated longing, hoarse at its edges, the prolonged velars of Ray Charles.

Glistening sheets of warm rain, the night silvered by ribbons of rain down the river, the first summer shower strung upon the radial glass, the downpour a glissando over the soundpost of steel, a spiral staircase descending from the bedroom loft to the open fireplace. Immense glazed windows looked out on the hedge that disguised the dike upon which Sam's house was built. In the winter, you could see the river through the willows. But the night Sam and Angela celebrated their thirteenth wedding anniversary, the river was veiled by shrubbery, and the world was a glass bubble you could tip over and stars would tumble and Ray Charles and a bit of champagne and Sam's tuxedo and Angela's pearl sequined dress and the shiver of rain across the tiles spilled splinters of pleasure over Angela's shoulders while they danced.

Angela leaned into Sam's throat to feel the vibrations of his voice. *They saaay, Ruby you're like a dreamme,* sang Ray Charles, and Sam said, they say, like a dream. *They saaay, Ruby you're like a songge, You just don't know right from wrongge.* And Sam said, right from wrong, heartaches for me.

They were home from an extravagantly dull party. Angela had soaked her hands with the broth that ran from the pink shells of boiled shrimp. Her tongue, she could feel it, white with the salt of caviar. And tortes, and those little meringues, blue cheese with grapes and the last sweet wine.

Sam smoothed Angela's sequined dress up, up over her wide hips, he cupped her breasts in each hand, Angela's breasts larger than his hand, he slipped the straps over her shoulders and slid the zipper down to the dimpled place in her broad back. With a certain force Sam pulled the dress over her breasts and her white soft belly to the red hair on her thighs to her feet which were bare when they danced. The skin, moist with summer heat, freckled on her chest and her round forearms. When she was naked Sam broke the waltz and he held Angela close, and he was only slightly taller but more in his black shoes and more by holding her tightly between his legs, Angela with her dimpled knees bending between Sam's long legs and he looked down into her eyes and taking a handful of Angela's red hair he pulled her head back and took her throat between his teeth and then he said, "How about something to eat, Angel." As Ray Charles and his strings, his piano, his horns, his bass, his subtle harp diminished, as the gospel choir shifted from major to minor, *She's but a dream,* as Sam laughed and released Angela to go up to his room, he told her, "I'm getting out of this monkey suit," climbing the spindled stairs. She stood naked, her white dress in her hands, her red hair fallen, in the quiver of light from melting candles on a glass table, in a trance from which Sam woke her when he leaned over the railing to say, "Angie. Food. Before I die."

Scrutiny

Angela was lucky in having what few people will ever enjoy, a profession that suited her temperament, like a talent, like an attribute, so she'd nearly had no choice in the matter. It was more an art than a career; if she weren't a lawyer she would be— what?—another woman with another name. Intuition was a habit that made her sensuous. She took things in through her pores, through the soles of her feet, with her back turned, apprehending. She could remember things in their entirety, an aerial view with infra-red film. Yet her interests rarely went further than a memory of surface features. She inhabited a world where the sum had little to do with its parts. That way, she could move between a truly sympathetic understanding of a case and a ruthless close-up of its technical features. She loved games, all kinds, could remember the rules of any card game she ever played, spit, cheat, or five card stud. Success was innate. Everybody said she was a good lawyer.

She slipped out of her shoes and crossed her chorus-girl legs, as if the broad table would protect her from view. The birthmark just above her right knee was evident through oyster-pale stockings. She'd been reading the newspaper; her fingertips and shirtsleeves were stained blue. From the back of the courtroom, Angela's eyes were theatrical, exaggerated by smudged mascara. The slack fatigue, the casualness, her distraction, lent her an attitude of confidence.

The Crown prosecutor was all circles, like a kid's drawing. A friend of Angela's, his name was Randy, but everybody called him No-Deal. He was short, wore a shiny grey suit, and rolled on his toes, hands in his pockets, a deferential smile on his dimpled face while he listened to the monotonous police officer. "At 1:07 a.m. myself and Officer Clinton accompanied the accused to the police cruiser."

"Did the accused say anything to you at that time, Officer?" asked No-Deal.

"Yes he did." Then the cop stopped, waiting for No-Deal's next line.

Randy stood, watching the cop, upstaging him. "Would you like to share that with us now?" Randy asked him softly.

"He began to ask for his lawyer." Indicating Angela, who gave a barely perceptible bow.

The courtroom had large wood doors that looked heavy but opened lightly, like a breath, letting in the smell of new carpet. Sam slipped into a seat at the back before the doors had shut. It was a large courtroom and gave him the crowded privacy he needed. She never looked back at the gallery.

The cop said, "May I read from my original notes made by myself at the time?"

Randy turned to the judge. "We've already established the specific relevance of the notes to this examination, your Honour."

Angela said that she had no objection.

"Proceed," said the judge.

The cop read with a slow monotone as if only recently literate. "The accused was asked by myself if the Magnum was loaded. The accused replied, 'No are you kidding I'd shoot my fucking foot off.'"

Then, a sudden triumph, No-Deal flourished a plastic bag before the judge. "Magnum serial number Z5617, your Honour, exhibit number twelve."

"Twelve?" asked the court recorder from her desk, stage left, just below the judge's dais. She adjusted the mike. She was having trouble tracing No-Deal's voice as he continued to move, standing in front of the policeman with his hands clasped like a worried mother, then pacing again in an area confined by the witness box and the table loaded with exhibits, the Magnum in its plastic bag, a semi-automatic, a Remington .22, one pink rubber glove, a pair of Foster Grant sunglasses, a black vinyl case with the gold Magnicom Spectra logo, a pair of black Levi jeans, a black leather belt with a plain silver buckle, a bottle of Party Boutique liquid make-up, a bottle of hydrogen peroxide, a curly brown wig, a black balaclava with red stitching around the eyes and a safety pin which loosely closed the mouth, several Lotto 6/49 tickets, and a pamphlet bearing instructions for hot-wiring a car.

The judge was a chubby, nearly blind man with Coke-bottle spectacles and bulging petulant eyes. Angela unfolded her legs, digging under the table for her shoes. It looked as if he were writing down her description. Sam had a nightmarish fear that the judge would charge Angie with a crime. She spoke to the police officer like the angel in the other ear.

ANGELA: You say you approached the home of Mrs. Seymore at 12:20 a.m. December twenty-third, is that correct?

COP: Uhh. Yes. Uhh, that is, yes.

ANGELA: He was alone in the house?

COP: Yes, alone.

ANGELA: You were alone with the accused from 12:20 until 1:09. Am I correct?

COP: Uhh, no. That would be 1:02, 3, we left the house and I escorted him to the police cruiser.

ANGELA: I see. You're not sure about the time. All right. Let's assume you left the house at 1:02. That gives you twenty-two minutes alone with the accused.

COP: Yes. Or, no. Mrs. Seymore was present.

7

"I'm sorry." Angela's breathy voice. "I must have misunder-stood you. Your initial statement led us to believe you were alone with the accused for twenty-two or maybe twenty-five minutes."

The cop flipped back through his notebook. For the first time, he looked at Angela; not at her face, but somewhere near her throat. Then he addressed the judge. "Your Honour, may I go to my jacket for my other notebook?"

The judge nodded, eyeglasses flashed his disapproval. Angela looked like she was waiting for a bus. Her necklace was turned backwards and the locket which had been Sam's recent gift was open and empty. The officer's jacket was draped over a chair in the second-last row of the gallery. Sam listened to him grunt and sigh while he searched the pockets. An ordinary man. Angela would underestimate the commonplace. She wasn't aware, now, that the judge was siding with the Crown prosecu-tor and the cop. She was too precious, too stylish, too canny for her own good.

She had lunch at the sprawling cafeteria with Randy and some defence attorneys, old friends from law school. Broccoli soup, tuna sandwich, a muffin, fries with gravy, strawberry jello with no whipped cream, and as an afterthought, the small salad. She loved these people. They'd played a lot of cards in school, but they were eggheads, head-of-the-class. Afflicted with high metabolism, they tilted their chairs and jiggled their feet, drummed their fingers on their saucers. Angela leaned toward them bumping their knees and pressing their shoulders. She always touched people while she talked to them. Her hearing wasn't good; things were too loud for her, and she couldn't dis-tinguish between ambient and salient noise.

They were teasing her for boring everybody over the tim-ing of the arrest. "You're just going to confuse the poor bas-tard and mess up his notes. Mix him up mess him up, that's Angie's style."

"The joy of defence counsel," Randy said. "You see total

8

stories break up into little icebergs, and then they just melt away into Stay of Proceeding Heaven." Randy was putting in his last days with the Crown before joining Angela's firm. Angela, the straight man, asked Randy when he would start at McClintoc McBurney McDuff.

"Going on a holiday first. A condo on Maui. We're renting a two-bedroom, two-bath, ocean-front condo. Make love in the Pacific's primordial embrace."

"Life of the rich and ugly," said Sharon.

Randy turned to Angela with masculine grace; Angie was tough, but she hadn't dispensed with her femininity like Sharon had. "As if I had a choice in the matter." Head back, he threw his gaze at Sharon. "I'm going to spend my potent years tied to my desk while the bank whips my ass. I'm so excited. One of my tax shelters just went bankrupt. I should stick to RRSPs. But they're not sexy. Angie's sexy. Defence is sexy." Lighting a cigarette, pudgy hands that would hold a martini, soon. He was balding, getting fat. Sharon said he looked like an '87 Chevy. But he loved women with a genuine gossipy affection. "I'll be popular like you, dear. Think your Magnum guy with the balaclava's gonna want me?" Angie draped her arm around him and gently massaged his neck. "If he doesn't, I could always stay home with a single light bulb and a can of sardines," he said. "I could spend more time with my kids." He let out a barklike laugh. "That'd scare the shit out of them."

Sharon yawned, an expression of affection. "Funny," she said (though it sounded like Fawwhanny), "I thought crime would go up in a recession."

"Domestic violence is way up." Everyone laughed at Randy's optimism.

Angela slapped Randy's hand away from her olive. Randy said, "Business ain't no better with the bear. Property crimes been good. Armed robbery. The odd big-bucks divorce." Randy wanted to go into corporate law, but he couldn't afford to make the switch out of criminal. It was too late for him.

"I don't want more crime. I just want more crooks to call me instead of going to that guy or that guy," Sharon said, and she pointed to Angela and Randy. Sharon had a broad soft-skinned face like a pansy.

They argued cheerfully, pushing plates away, lighting cigarettes. Angela looked as if she were having a pleasant dream, her eyes half-closed, her cheek shoved into her left hand. She was like a delinquent teenager. Sam approached their table before anyone noticed, like an owl in the woods. He reached around and put his hands around Angie's throat and gave her a squeeze. Randy didn't recognize Sam at first, and when Angela yelled Randy pushed his chair back and, after a brief lapse, put his fists up. Everyone laughed and Sam winced and said, "She's my wife." They looked at him then as they would look at a stranger. Sam steadied himself on Angela's chair. His height felt excessive; he looked a long way down at his white hand, then into Angela's familiar face. Her fear had been there somehow before he'd pulled it out and Sam wondered who had placed it so deep that it could precede him. She was catching her breath now. She really did look relieved to see him, blushing and excited. "I was just in the building," he said to her.

Quickly, to efface the embarrassment, they made him welcome. Sharon said, "Now I know why she's always thinking about you." Sam half-smiled. Angela claimed him, her pleasure abundant and real. "We were talking about the new inquiry," she said. "Come and help me defend myself against Randy."

"It is my opinion that it's a prolific piece of shit," said Randy.

Angela touched her husband's arm. "I think Sam was offended by the kind of fictional style of the first one. He thinks the new one's an improvement. Don't you babe?" To Sharon, "It's nice he reads this stuff." Angela would translate Sam for other people. His unusual appearance and his diffidence sometimes put people off, and she was anxious to defend him or explain him to people.

"It's nothing but a goddamn backlash." Randy got up. "Anyway, nice seeing you. I've got to run. Aggravated assault at 2:30. Bye Ange. See you at the conventional lawyers' drunk."

Sam shook Randy's hand, held it briefly, said, "Conventional drunk?"

"He means the convention next weekend. I told you about it," Angela said.

"No you didn't, Angie, you forgot. I guess she forgot. It doesn't matter."

Randy bit Sharon's earlobe. "Bye glamourpuss."

"Fuck off," said Sharon.

It appeared that Randy had no romantic interest in Angela after all. He was too relaxed, he didn't seem ruffled. Sam was suddenly interested. He stopped Randy. "Why do you think the inquiry's a piece of shit?" It was strange when Sam would swear, like he was imitating somebody.

Randy bowed again to Angela and said, "Your husband seeks my opinion. I think the government has a vested interest in keeping the courts running smoothly, which in this case means they want the jails full of Indians, and the legal profession full of intense young Jews like yours truly."

Sam hadn't realized Randy was Jewish.

"I hadn't realized you were a lefty."

"Sure. I'm a fucking Marxist."

Angela scraped the rest of the butter out of its plastic container and sucking her finger she said, "I think Randy's referring to poverty crime, Sam."

"Whatever. It's systemic. And the current regime wants to keep it that way. At any rate, I'm late."

Sharon was trying to read the screen on her daytimer. "You are a hypocrite from hell, Randy boy."

Randy patted her shoulder. He glanced at his watch. It was perhaps the twelfth time he'd done that. But his preoccupation was real and it didn't seem to have much to do with Angela.

a scrutiny he calls love

They were nighthawks. They drank dry white, but they never had a hangover, though sometimes their eyes when they woke were fervid and over-clear. Angela and Sam would wake very early, everything about them sweet with citrus, a clean burn, a pure fermentation.

They had married when they were in their mid-twenties, though Sam was a few years older. It had been the most natural thing in the world. In the first few years of their marriage, Sam and Angie had travelled a lot, photographed each other in bleached Mediterranean sunlight. Luxury made them seem healthy. Once when they were skiing in Switzerland, Angela was driving the rented Jeep and she felt muscular and it had been a day free of all expressions of gravity, her body in perfect condition, completely unfettered by age, children, necessity. Beyond that, she loved to drive a good car. They'd skied hard all day. The moist winter air was full of voices. Lights from the chalets glowed in the valley and the dusk was the colour of blue spruce. They sat in a pine room that smelled of snow and firewood, full of American families. Angela was too hungry to care for the first while. She ate the bread and cheese with wine. She was happy so she sang while she ate, and when she met Sam's eye, she chewed and smiled and hummed. At the table beside them, two children were kicking at each other with their dress-up patent shoes. They revealed their bottom teeth, fighting viciously, secretively, while their parents fingered their wine glasses and gazed about the room looking for something to say. Beneath a deckled sweater, the woman was nursing a baby. Angela spoke to Sam, a conspirator. "I'm always glad were not somebody else." She looked at the bland comfort of the family. She shivered. "Let's never change."

"I think she looks beautiful," said Sam, indicating the nursing mother.

It took Angie by surprise. "Yeah?" Considering. "What? The sweater?" Turning to him, flushed with sun and wine. "If it's rhinestones you want baby . . ."

Perhaps that was the first time Sam narrowed himself into a long thin solemn line, his face utterly serious and confident and right. "A mother is the most beautiful thing in the world," he said.

It would have seemed altogether corny to promise him a baby right then and there, but she had taken him to a hotel, oiled him, bedded him, and eventually she whispered that she'd like a child, turning a promise into an act of seduction which made Angela feel less obedient. Sam seemed to relax; she thought she'd smoothed away his new hesitancy.

But it grew, Sam's refuge from Angela, slowly, so she felt she was making it up. He was always willing to be with her, and it was obvious that he loved her with his new fatalistic determination. She grew to understand that she was nervous and needed reassurance to an excessive degree.

In their history there was only one other moment when his retreat was visible, a moment as errant as dinner in Switzerland. They were on a beach, a blue night, they could see each other by the light clothes they wore, and the breeze blew Angela's white scarf, and Sam had looked at her and what he saw was

13

Angela being seen by him, Angela being seen, and the abrupt solitude that claimed him stayed. He had walked a little away from her, Angela would remember it this way because the distance and their parallel paths gave her a lovely sense of mutual independence. She would often remark to her women friends that she and Sam were free because they lived inside a large marriage, like a very big house, and she loved the freedom of her house arrest. Sam was like a man learning to hide the indications of his own breathing. It made him seem invulnerable. Angela grew to count on that.

When he touched her, his hands were familiar and challenging, as if they were making an impossible claim. Angela proved compliant, smiling a little while he manipulated her with his hands. She enjoyed his admiration. She would try to make him whisper, but he loved her with his hands, with his eyes which were serious, a little sad. He was free to look at her; she posed for him and he made love to her as if proving the unprovable. Angela wasn't wrong to think this was the infinite beginning of married love. It would be several years before he'd gone beyond her reach so when she dropped her kisses onto his smooth surface they fell right through, as if he hadn't witnessed or didn't believe. Her loving would leave him hungry. He continued to stroke her white round body but when she reached for him he took her hands and put them back upon her own skin, and he would watch her caress herself. Angela would sleep and in the morning there would be no words for it, and she still assumed it was his desire, a false transaction, yet a temporary detour in their long affair. He would be back, she would wait, and in the meantime, she enjoyed being watched by Sam because he loved her.

Home

Summer affected the city like creeping amnesia, everyone for-getting they had to earn a living. Angela was working less, or rather, as she preferred, she was working more at home. Weekends had grown fat, spreading themselves over four som-nolent days.

It was Friday. Angie and Sam had slept past eight. In the pale green light of a cloudy summer day, they woke, belated and vaguely repentant and aware of the gentle lapping of their own voices, how one would hear them from the outside, a man and woman waking to their secret lives, the nuance bleached from our hearing. Sam's muscular shoulder, her hand on his throat, dipping into the hollow formed by his collarbone. There would never be an end to her hand on his skin.

Angela's garden was windswept. It lay precariously on the fractured ledge above the river where it twisted, prevented from final erosion by tufted shrub and the willows that grew up around it. But today there was no wind. And a cloud cover lay so it was haze feathering the edges of things. Sam had built a dock below the garden, and the river being low that year, its cribbing rested partially on the baked grey mud.

Angela tossed weeds into a corner of the garden, she rolled mosquitoes against her legs. Then it was past noon and the ceramic daylight nearly too hot for such labour. Her fingers ached from the calcified soil and the powdered juice from plants dried on her hands. The pump droned lazily from the river. She was always uncertain about river water, how acidic it felt, though doubtless it was her own sweat made it sting like that. Sam heard her laughing when it caught her.

He was sitting at the end of the dock. Sam had a peculiar way of sitting with his bare feet flat and his knees up on either side, an ancient posture, lithe, an arrangement of surfaces and planes. Sam's long limbs telescoped, at rest, he folded his arms between his knees, holding a cigarette, flicking with his thumb the neat white ash.

Dark irises from equatorial regions filter the sunlight but Sam was from a northern climate and his eyes were the colour of snow in shade, his eyes let in more light. His hair was crow-black and his skin was pale and this lent Sam's eyes a milky illumination. He was very tall and his hands were fine and long. He loved to dress well. Even today while he worked outside he wore an old expensive shirt open on his chest and grey cotton shorts that rode his hips. He was a strangely beautiful man even in disarray.

The sun was a wafer, flat and dry. Angela levered herself onto the back porch and sat swinging her feet, the top half of her torso in shadow. She carried with her the fragrance of cut grass. She had tied up her hair to cool her throat and there was mud creased in the nape of her neck. The screen door, painted green, took her into a back entrance where Sam followed. She dropped her muddy gloves and sandals and went inside.

The house was still, absolute, the air mauve and thick with heat. Sam's was a celebrated house, though strangers rarely saw it. A self-taught architect, Sam had designed it himself. It was massive, almost entirely glass and steel, a structure of startling transparency. From the driveway you could see the stone fireplace, the high cedar ceilings, the staircase that spiralled to a loft. It was fascinating because so much was visible and it seemed to have no boundaries, its edges blurred with the trees that surrounded it, shining the sky back upon itself. The glass attested to the privilege of privacy which Sam had acquired when he built it on ten acres of wooded land, an oxbow formed by the river. There was no one around so Sam was free to look out on the blown woods, the wind full of seeds.

In this house Angela spent much of her time. Her office was at the top of the staircase beside their bedroom. Coming in from the garden, she could see up to her desk and a mess of paper because she had been preparing for a trial. Weary and hot, she stretched out in front of the fireplace on a Navajo rug dyed with iron oxide, woven in various shades of red, rested her head on pillows, Angela's hair like fireweed, her skin firm as if it wouldn't touch or be touched. She had a nimbus, a silent space between flesh and world, between her limbs and the endless afternoon. Sam watching her smiled because the slender differences in weave, hair, lips would be invisible to Angela who was marked with the peculiarity of colour-blindness, a rare event in a woman but she was truly blind to variations in red. She had always been blind to red.

Despite that, Angela's vision was otherwise very good. She lay recovering from the heat, and her eyes were like hands on Braille, reading the infinite details of Sam's accumulation of *objets d'art*. Sam owned Import Trade, an upscale wholesaler catering to the consumption of Third World products. He supplied hotels in Hawaii with baskets handwoven by women in Thailand, and shopping malls in North Dakota with pink and turquoise Guatemalan weaves and with oily sweaters knit by ten-year-old girls in Equador. Sam would fly to Equador and rent a white Lincoln. He seemed to enjoy aggressive bad taste when he was alone, would wear white eel-skin shoes, came home once with black nail polish on one hand. "You'll get murdered some day," said Angela, not only afraid for him, uneasy for other reasons.

He would drive to the villages and watch the blur of the

girls' hands when they knit. When he returned home he would tell Angela that they moved fast as hummingbirds. She liked that, the hummingbirds. He'd stay in tourist compounds, swimming in the pool every morning, sleeping on sheets washed by peasants, "like a Nazi in exile," Angie told him, trying to be tender. Even the rich tourists left him alone. But Angela knew that in such circumstances, Sam would live a Spartan life in the sense that he travelled with no illusions and while he bought at times a half million dollars' worth of goods, he never acquired any tangible methods of curing his isolation. He worked hard and at night he returned to his hotel bed early, sober, lucid to his homelessness. Angela had become so accustomed to the channelling of international trade through her husband's hands, she had over the years come to assume that he was central to the world, a kind of domestic reversal of the Copernican revolution.

Sam used to travel all the time. For business he bought the status quo. But for home, his taste was eclectic. He had chosen on his travels the paintings, tapestries, lamps, grass baskets, pistols, a delicate cane chair, carved maple boxes, impasto ceramics, glass miniatures, ebony bowls, shaman masks, eighteenth-century porcelain figures, Chinese neolithic water jars, a ram-shaped aquamarine of buffware with a green glaze decorated with pellets, discreet and intricate, gnomic, silent, autotelic. Each object was sufficient unto itself. Every object worthy of devotion. She counted these things as part of herself, as if in looking at Sam's tasteful acquisitions she were looking at her own portrait.

Sam's worship was taxonomic. He had made an inventory of his house. He had a method of classification more sophisticated than the International Harmonized System, more sensitive than Canada Customs. Beyond the international six-digit code, beyond the additional four digits peculiar to Canada, beyond the Harmonized System which will determine the essential character of each item according to its country of origin, its bulk, quantity, value, use, beyond ten determinate digits, Sam's system began with a break, like an ellipsis or a caesura in a poem, after which he predicated a personal reading of his possessions with a surd, an irrational root, purely subjective, closed to anyone but himself. Sam's cyphers were stored only on disk, an e-file accessible through his own PIN. Many nights Angela would find him lit by his amber monitor, Sam admiring his possessions through their numeric identity, their ideal codification.

She was lying in his shade. Looked up, could see him, purple silhouette, when he moved, sun in her eyes. "I'm tired," she said. Then, casual, a drawl, "I have to go out tonight."

"Oh yeah," said Sam, halfway to a question.

"The girls are asking me for dinner. I've said no so often, I just can't again tonight." She lay back, feeling hungry. "I'm so tired," again.

"Why's that?" He went to the kitchen and opened the fridge. Angie stood, followed.

She stopped his hand on the fridge door. "That's a bit obvious." And Sam, mercifully, smiled. They stood before the open fridge and appraised the crystal bowls wrapped in Saran she'd left there since the last dinner party. He poured a drink.

She always tried to let him know, carefully, the details of her absences and her reluctance to be away from him. The girls were playing tennis at 6:30. Doubles. Sharon and Regina and some woman from Sharon's office who is apparently a real bitch but hot at the net.

"But the weird part is," said Angie, "we're going swimming after that."

"That's weird, is it?" asked Sam, flat voice.

"Well it's just, we're going swimming at the pits."

He looked blank.

"The gravel pits," she said. "You know where I met you. Out by Bird's Hill."

He walked from the counter to the couch and stood looking out, sipping. "That will be nice."

"A pain in the neck," she said, stretching. "I really don't feel like it."

She joined him, wrapped her leg up around the shelf of his pelvis. "I remember hating you. You were with those chicks with their tits showing. I thought you'd be decadent." She tongued his throat. "Why would I think something like that? Dumb, yes?"

Sam agreed, kissing her, yes, dumb, and the laughter real in him at last, so real she was truly sorry to leave just a little later and they were lying together now on the red rug for a long time listening to her friends hooting at her from the driveway. "Hey!" It was Regina's voice. "Hey! Bitch!" Regina yelled. "You get the east court!"

"Who are you balling in there?" Sharon, in a rare and raucous mood.

"Balling!" Regina twisted around from the driver's seat to scrutinize her friend. "What planet? Sometimes I can't believe I even know you."

Sam came outside. He was standing at the car before anyone realized.

"Oh hi Sam," said Sharon from the back seat. Regina was still looking back and she thought Sharon was kidding. Regina said, "Oh sure. Sam would come out here and inspect the getaway car." Then she turned and saw him, her head fell back, her mouth wide open and her large teeth showing, her laugh like a ribbon pulled out of her spine. Then she jumped out from behind the wheel, bare knees and feet bony and perpendicular, she wrapped herself around him, an imitation of Angela that was uncanny, because Regina was like a parody of Angela, skinny and crisp. Sam was unmoved. He nearly pushed her off but he didn't, his hands stayed limp at his sides.

When Angela raised her head from the pillows the loud sun pushed and filled her ears, her mouth, heat in her head. It was nearly six. Sam came inside and put on a CD so loud she couldn't talk. Jazz. Nervous stuff. She washed her neck. She dressed to go. Looked outside. "Hey bitch! Hurry up you dumb cow!" Angie told them to wait and she made a thick tuna sandwich with slices of avocado and thin slices of lemon peel. Sam read a magazine on the couch, Charlie Parker on so loud he couldn't hear her say goodbye. She was eating when she slid into the car beside Sharon, Sharon saying, You're going to eat that whole thing and then play tennis? And Angie saying, Fuckin' right. "Oooo, *some*body's in a bad mood." Angela looked out the window as the maple trees in Sam's driveway went fast in reverse. She could see herself in the car window, the outline of her white pointed nose, sun shining on particles of dust and summer pollen, planes of Angela's face in double exposure with the green foliage, lawn, crew-cut hedge, polaroid summer, bright green stink of sun.

May

Angela's mother was called May. She had lived alone in a modest-seeming brick bungalow not far from Sam's house since her husband had died, twelve years ago. She wore her silver hair long and pinned with wide hairpins. She was buxom and steady and liked to be alone. At whatever hour you approached her, you found her well dressed, a trace of lipstick, cornflower shadow to enunciate her cornflower eyes. She had famous hands which she cared for, polishing her nails with a nearly clear polish so the whites were firmly shaped. But in the last ten years the arthritis had contracted the lumbrical muscles, inflamed the knuckles, till the long splayed painter's fingers resembled the whitened body of a toad on the road. That is how May described them. She took aspirin for the pain; an inadequate analgesic but May preferred clarity to comfort.

When her hands were finally rendered useless, May grew devoted to music. She hated noise and was acutely sensitive to sound. Her listening was intense and miniature. She would listen, seated on a kitchen chair placed between small black speakers. She placed her feet flat on the floor and sat straight and she listened with her own diaphragm. Music informed May, her high-boned face alert, compassionate.

The house was full of her paintings. May had favoured thick, leafy colours. She had been a success in Europe, but not at home where taste required more obvious difficulty, gaiety more muted. She was considered too feminine, an amateur, though she was plagued by the pilgrimages of Parisian graduate students who considered her the painterly equivalent of Gertrude Stein.

Her most popular work had been on tour for ten years and had recently been elevated to calendar status in the United States. But Angela's favourite was uncharacteristically representational and, it was often remarked, parodic and fractured in its theme if not in its execution. An oil, in colours womanly and springlike, redundant, a depiction of a woman seated at a desk before a window overlooking a garden; she wears a dress fragile as a yellow petal and of the Directoire period, a woman graciously unfocused, posed as if she would be writing but her attention is compelled by the painter, whom we see over-the-shoulder, a filmic perspective, his dun-coloured arm extended, and we see him from an adjoining room which is perhaps the woman's nursery because the French windows are painted lemon yellow and if we look very closely we can see they are closed so the painting is a series of collapsing frames and glass upon glass upon glass. A visual cliché, except that the woman eludes definition. Object of desire, instigator, transgressor, enigma.

The subject of many scholarly essays, the cover on at least two anthologies on the female body and cultural representation, the painting is also testimony to May's devotion to Angela. May painted it when Angela was only ten, but she had studied Angela's crimson cheeks one summer as the child lay sleeping and she saw her as she would be as a mature woman and so began the many studies of the child as a woman and Angela and May had in various ways been the same age ever since. When the child Angela saw the painting, she had asked her mother,

What is she writing? May had replied, It's just a letter to a friend. Who is the painter? young Angela asked. And May had told her that he was a friend of the woman's husband. Was the painter in love with the woman writing? The painter? Yes, he was in love with this woman, the wife of his friend. Isn't that a sin? asked the child Angela, who knew sin as a black word with wings. No, her mother told her, it wasn't a passionate love, he simply enjoyed his desire for his friend's wife. And so the child learned desire. The colours of this painting, morning, womanhood, maternal, yet the painter sees her lit by sun, seated at a desk by a window which frames the garden. She is a woman at her desk on a day the sun and wind crack spring wide open. It was a still life, but shattered by the reciprocal, infinite relay of the lovers' glance.

And later, Angela as a young woman leaving home saw for the first time it wasn't a letter she was writing. It was a journal, a journal of aphorisms. She was writing a diary of temptation. And that is when Angela began to keep one for herself.

Sam's Birthday

Angela and Regina sat down together, throwing their heads back in laughter so you could see their pink palates, the pale blue lines in their throats. "Exactly!" they cried and they wiped tears from the corners of their eyes. "Happy birthday Sammy!" said Regina. Sam suffered a kiss, his arms full of dishes. "What a perfect husband, isn't he a *per*fect husband?" This, directed to Angela. Suddenly serious, Angie agreed, yes, perfect. Regina's face was smiling but her eyes were sober, watching Angela kiss Sam and then disarm him. Like a man falling from stilts, Sam folded his long waist and sneezed, it would appear, on his shoes. "Sam," Angela said. "You don't do dishes on your birthday." Ethel the maid levered a tray of shrimp upon her commodious hips. "I'll do that," Ethel said, and her thick palm balanced all while she rolled away as if she were on ball bearings. Angela looked helpless, discovered the cakes cut and ready to be eaten. Her joy returning, she put her fingers in the whipping cream and went to find somebody to talk to.

There were many slender women with bare collarbones and

men's ties loose and trays of glasses passing overhead. Angela moored at the edge of a conversation about criminal defence. She had invited some people from work. Regina was telling a joke, the voice like shale upon a bed of irony, drifting carelessly in and out of a brogue. "So, suddenly, he's out planting a rock garden, day after day, busy planting this incredible garden see? And he tells the police, 'Auchch, she's run off wi' the milkman,' you see. And this little dog is yapping." Regina's freckle-coloured hair was pinned to her head, as if she'd forgotten to brush it after a bath. She was dressed in a strapless pink brocade, a debutante. Her audience, parked in a semicircle, smiled with their lips shut. Regina reached one periscopic arm for a glass and destroyed her own joke. "You see he'd cut her up into little tiny pieces and he'd wrapped up each little piece, like meals for one, very carefully you know, in plastic. Then he buried each piece separately." Her audience moaned and then they drifted to the food. "Meals for one!" she called after them.

Regina caught Angela's arm and pulled her to the couch where Sharon sat, stalwart and nearsighted and contented. Sharon blandly acknowledged her friends and said, "I was just thinking about what I read today in the dictionary."

"Don't spare us."

Sharon nodded, duly encouraged. "I was looking up the word *lethality*."

"That's not a word," said Regina.

"It is."

Angela leaned into Sharon's shoulder, watching the lines come and go in her square face.

Sharon said, "But what I found was *leprosy*."

"That's nice, you hag. Scintillating. Let's go." Regina seized Angie's hand. Angela retained it and nestled further into Sharon's unyielding shoulder, squeezed between her friends. Regina sneezed, loudly, a full-bodied sneeze, and she said, "Oh I love it when that happens." She pinched Angela's arm. "You do that for me baby."

"It reminded me of something," said Sharon.

"Adolescence," said Angela.

"*Scrofula.* Now there's a word. You want to talk words, let's talk *scrofula.* Or its plural. *Scrofulae.*" Regina's voice was improved by cigarettes. And she was a skilled drinker, a power drinker, somehow liquor made her resonant. "*Scrofulatum. Scrofulant.*"

Sharon nodded. "It reminded me of something a friend who travelled in Africa had once told me."

"Lepers make good lovers," said Regina, triumphant.

Sharon in dismay. "How did you know?"

"God, Sharon, you told that one already. You don't remember? Lepers make the best lovers. Nobody can love like one. They can't get enough. They're desperate to touch and be touched. She doesn't remember. She drinks and forgets."

"Ignore her," said Sharon to Angela.

"What *is* this obsession with numb erotics?"

"I am a contemporary woman. I've got something to tell you, Regina. Eisenhower is not president. My erotics are not numb. They are hypothetical. Welcome to the nineties."

Regina, suddenly affectionate, kissing them both, said, "That reminds me! I had this dream last night. There was this flying wizard, a bearded man in a sea-blue robe who flew up over my head and he was so kind and wise, I think I was seeing my Guardian, and he said, 'Have clarity! Life is by proxy!' "

"You think you have a Guardian? Now she's New Age."

"You know what was really strange about my dream? It's exactly like what you're saying," and she stroked Sharon's straight brown hair. "Everything is prophylactic."

"Well I should hope so."

Angela could feel her eyes, the rings around them, the way time ornaments a face.

It was late and the people with children would soon go home. Angela had a surprise for Sam which she wanted to reveal. She called for their attention. The party was overripe, her voice drowning in babble. Randy rescued her by fetching the dinner gong, British-Hong Kong. He mimed an immense gesture toward smashing it with both arms and yelled, GONGGGG! Everyone offered their flushed faces.

"Oh shit," she said, "I shouldn't be standing here. Wait everybody!" She disappeared into the back pantry, a moment devoid of dramatic intention.

Angela had placed Sam's gift on a patio table which she manoeuvred through the folding doors, over the tiled kitchen and onto the rug. When she plugged it in, it bubbled, throaty and self-contained, and threw green light over Angela's dress. Through the watergrass darted shining neon fish. "Ahhhh," said the party and they applauded. "Where's Sam?"

Where is Sam? And then Sam appearing behind Angela, smiling cautiously. "This is for me? More dependants?"

Angela's refrain; even as she was saying it, she wondered why she was being so repetitious. "Oh shit," she said. "Poor Sam, no. I'll look after them."

Regina called out, "Oh for christsake Sammy! Lighten up!"

"It's beautiful!"

"That's fifty? It's a fifty, right? Saltwater tank?"

The party gathered to admire Sam's new aquarium but Sam stopped them then and said, "I have a gift for Angela." He reached into his jacket and took out a slim box. "Oh no Sam, not again," said Angela. The party demanded she open it at once. From the small blue box she withdrew a ruby brooch set with diamonds. The sound of merriment fell away. Angela looked into its crystalline points. She had a feeling of highway, the rough cut of road she had passed over quickly in Sam's red Triumph with the side-curtains off and the highway very close and the surface of asphalt but Angela was stationary, contradicting speed.

Everyone left at once. "Looks like a funeral," said Angie, watching the headlights flicker through the trees, a procession of Mercedes Benz. Would be a wealthy corpse. "What's the plural of Benz?" She turned to him, Sam on the couch staring at the ceiling. She traced a path to the ceiling. Oh. Saw themselves in the glass. He'd been looking at her. "Benzi," she said, hummed while she flipped big marble ashtrays into a garbage bag, butts and bottle caps and silver wrapping from champagne, matches, an earring, which she chucked, cheap thing, never saw it. Wanting Ethel to fill the dishwasher and go. After a party, remove all traces of human life. Sound of another breathing. Clear away the whole house if she could, lift up one end and let every couch and ornament fall into a great plastic bag, paintings fall from their walls, clear the ashes from the fireplace, let Ethel roll inside, tie it tight, put it outside.

"Ethel!" Angie went to the kitchen, stood beside the fat woman, secretly letting her arm touch Ethel's soft plump elbow, her cool skin. "Sam called a cab for you. I'll finish up tomorrow." Ethel looked at her. Behind the friendship, an edge of distaste in the yellow eyes. Angela handed her a couple of hundred dollars. Ethel shuffled to her purse and was gone.

Still he lay on the couch. She turned down the lights. Efface the reflection. She wished he'd fall asleep. "Did you have a nice time at your party?" Sam asked.

"It was supposed to be for you."

"That's all right. I'm too old for a birthday party. Everybody comes to see you."

It was too stupid to argue over who likes whom. Three a.m. She went to bed and slept thick and a little sick from wine. She didn't hear him come in. But woke to hear him outside their room. It was still dark outside. She heard his determined breathing, and scraping furniture. She went in the dark to see. Sam had already moved the two bedside tables, rolled a small rug and placed it on top, was then fitting a lamp beside it, the cord carefully wrapped and tied to its base. "What are you doing?"

He didn't hear. His eyes were open with a focus more intense than in his waking self, but he didn't see. His body looked old. The strength he showed was in the effort, not vigorous but concentrated. She touched his arm and could feel the drive forward to his task. And was afraid, fear curling her tongue, taste of iron, rust in her mouth cooked by fear. His head, bent to the job, would move all the furniture to the hallway, pile it up. "Sam. You're asleep."

He looked at her, seeing her in his sleep, fact of his hate flat in his eyes. Without waking, went to bed.

She returned the furniture to their room, making a lot of noise, not caring if she woke him. He lay in bed and didn't move. In the morning, she told him what he'd done. He said she had been dreaming, she'd kept waking him last night with her tossing about. It was like that when she drank. Just the way she was. They glanced at each other, walleyed.

But it wasn't many days before he cleared up and the off-hand comments on his age stopped and he seemed to fit within himself once again and his peculiarities didn't matter because he always had Angela and with her at home he didn't need anyone else.

The Revenant

Sam had told Angela this story which became for her Sam's signature.
Or more, his lyric, a reason for loving the sound of his footsteps, his
breathing, his hands on the arm of a chair, his indifferent back when
he wasn't aware of her watching.

The girl lived in a high white stucco block pitched into sand and
grass, mazy with flies. The walls were slabs of sunlight washed
watery pink or pale sienna depending on the hour. The heat was
intense that summer. Buildings tilted and the rare cloud,
smudged and stock still. The girl seemed older than Sam because
she had orphaned herself and kept a queer pain balanced without remorse within her narrow body. She was as black-haired as
he was and they were twinned by their height and their winter-
coloured eyes. They talked about things far away, the distant
future when they would individually re-enter the world, the time
after this inchoate summer. Mostly, they stayed apart like binary
stars, she in her white-hot cell, he in his wood cabin in a grove

of birch by the lake. The sun lay like a cataract on the water, bleaching driftwood, yellow grass, blanched and still, and when he walked on the sand there were dead fishflies cool underfoot. It was Sam's peculiar romance. She was his match, apprehensive and cool, rapid and utterly at rest, ancient, arrogant, young. They smoked cigarettes and grass in the afternoon, their conversation exhaled smoke. They were learning to live without money and food. Both pretended they had never been children; they had always been this cool, this stoned, this hungry, this indifferent to hunger. Their ambivalence was insatiable.

She began to take little white pills, to be calm. Sam watched from shore while she drifted out on a synthetic breeze. His respect for her grew with her distance from him. When she was most neglectful, he was more nearly in love. But it was more innate than love; a thirst for the girl's departure.

He began to care for her when she had quite stopped feeding herself; when the cigarettes burned worm-holes in her shirts, he would walk through the shadows of trees and across the glaring sand dunes to her flat. It was August by then. The late summer winds had come up, full of sand drilling a face on the rocks on shore. She was listless and honest and bland with him with a casual, ersatz domesticity. She would spill tea down herself and change in front of him, revealing a body neither muscled nor fleshy, the pure lines of a fish, an abstraction, breast, pelvis, her lovely feet, the shade of her dark-haired body. The white wood door remained open between bed and bath. She was music drifting through.

Sam had a way of provoking a story, short of its telling, an extemporaneous method, to skim the surface of his memory. Sam and Angela shared the affliction of nostalgia, but Sam enjoyed it like he enjoyed his nicotine. He never told it as tragedy with tragic consequence. The girl's poverty, like Sam's, was temporized with family money. Everything was improbable. It would seem she had a child hidden with parents somewhere else on a coast. She was a creature of another species, a hawk-moth, wings opened in the dark. Her failure, her fast deceleration, was refined beyond judgement.

When she fell from the roof of her apartment it was either very late or very early on a late summer night. Either way the sky remained lead-paned, cathedral blue. Angela didn't know if he saw her fall. Angela saw her fall, like a doll in the air. But she never saw her fallen. She would ask Sam often for the story, when they were intimate and resting, knowing that it would end with the girl in mid-air, with the iteration of Sam's admiring glance.

Patrick

Patrick had exaggerated poise, elaborately graceful mannerisms and a rapacious sense of self-importance. He entered the interview room like Fred Astaire on his way to meet Cyd Charisse. He swung his arms in careful semicircles, he *strolled,* toes pointed out, whistling under his breath. He pulled his pant legs up a little above the knees and was seated, his hands folded before him on the table, when Angela arrived.

She was no lawyer, that much was obvious. There was much that was obvious about Angela. Judging from the size of her, she would be a woman who liked ice cream. When Patrick greeted Angela he was thinking about pistachio, about cherry burgundy. When he rose to offer her his slender hand (she enveloped Patrick's hand, a sculptor greeting a young pianist) he was remembering Italian ice. He studied Angela's pimento-coloured hair (it was the fluorescent light, suppressed the tawny) and he recalled the old woman who sold him gelati, her sleek black hair, her diamond-shaped face when she smiled and stood on her toes to reach over the glass counter.

Angela threw her briefcase on the table and removed her suit jacket. "Whew! Aren't you dying?" She wore a sleeveless white shirt which revealed her arms, round and freckled.

Patrick followed the freckles on Angela's arms like a traveller in a field of poppies, his eyes suddenly aching to sleep, the dream of the ice cream woman threatening to overwhelm him. He focused on her eyes, green. He abruptly sneezed.

"Are you OK?" she asked.

"Sure. I'm fine."

"That's really weird," she said quietly.

"What's that?"

"Oh, nothing, it's just—" She waved her marble arms. "I wonder if I make people allergic."

Again, Patrick fought to keep his eyes from rolling back in his head. To sleep, to sleep. She was nodding at the cop in the observation window. "Nice guy," she said.

"I guess so."

"Have you made a statement?" When she looked worried she made little reindeer antlers between her eyes.

"I think so. I told them what happened, sort of. They caught me red-handed." His laughter was charming, boyish and affable. "I've always wanted to say that. Red-handed."

"How old are you, Patrick?"

"Twenty-six."

"Why were you in her house?"

"I don't know. It's something I like to do."

Baffled, she blew out a breath. Patrick nodded slightly, identifying the smell of maraschino. "How could you not, like, know?" she asked.

"Well I walked in the front door, if that's what you mean. It was open." When Angela appeared to be disappointed, Patrick looked for something to give her. He said patiently, as if he were much older than she was, "You're wondering whether there was forethought. There wasn't."

"Are you a student?"

"Self-taught." The smile.

"Did you know the woman?"

35

"Not really. I'd seen her."

"You watched her?"

"Sort of. I'm not a pervert. I'd passed her house all the time and she'd be in her garden. She planted a lot of flowers back there. It was nice."

"Patrick, did you go to her house to steal?"

"No no. I don't need anything. The cops think I was there to steal. They have no imagination. Really." And he laughed.

"Well, it's tough when you were going through her things like that."

"I look. I don't touch." He showed her his palms. His eyes were smiling. He was good-natured.

"Did you know she was home?"

"I did and I didn't." He drew this for her, turning his hands over, *comme ci comme ça.* "If I'd known she was home, it would imply that I had a plan, do you see? And it wasn't like that. I simply went in on a whim. It's a dare with myself." Shrugged. "Hard to explain."

Angela was watching him, interested, so he continued.

"It's the kind of thing everybody wants to do. I looked in through the front window. It was hot and sunny so it was hard to see much because of the trees on the window."

"Pardon?"

"The trees on the window."

"Oh. The reflection."

"She has this black gate, kind of ritzy, but you know suburbs, all the houses the same, except for this gate, all fancy. She left the front door open too, like an invitation. I just walk into her house." He shook his head in self-deprecating wonder. "It's cool inside. And it smells good, like floor polish. But she must be some kind of wild woman. She'd be a terrible mother, that's my opinion. It's good she doesn't have kids."

It would happen whenever Angela became aware that people are a little crazy. She'd be paying attention and then there would be that moment when she recognized that what they were telling her was completely off the wall. She would suddenly lose her bearings; it was like a picture slipping out of its frame and landing lopsided on the floor. It was very hard to remember strange occurrences, and it was impossible to know whether people were really nuts or if she was just naive. It was the same when someone would tell her a joke; the funnier the joke, the less likely was she to remember it. She was often amazed and went into shock easily.

"The place was a mess," said Patrick. "Clothes all over the place. Hanging on the doors, and in the dining room, you know where a family would sit down and eat." Patrick showed Angela how the family would sit, drawing boxes with his hands. "Shiny silver material. On the table, see? She must have been making a Halloween costume, a robot costume or a ballerina if it was for a little girl. Why she would be making a Halloween costume in June is anybody's guess. There was a sewing machine right there where the family would eat. She was sewing something. Obviously."

"Then she found you?"

"She came downstairs. It was fine at first. I wasn't scared. Not at all. It was such a nice day." He looked up at the ceiling which was plexiglass. His shoulders tipped right and left. Angela watched his muscled shoulders move beneath a fine linen shirt, a rich ochre colour. He pointed up with his right hand. He wore a ring, not garish, silver with a coral-coloured stone. "She came walking down the stairs, getting bigger all the time."

"She came into view."

"Her foot and then her knees and then her whole leg." Patrick smiled pleasantly. "The whole shebang."

"Was she frightened?"

"Her throat made a funny noise. You know like a cat before it's going to be sick? A screw-up in communication."

Angela's stomach spoke one long circuitous sentence. It went on so long, it had to be acknowledged. She looked from her belly to Patrick and shrugged. Patrick politely held there, waiting.

"That was all right with me I guess. A bit strange. I can see it from her perspective. You're a woman," he said. Angela crossed her legs, easing herself in her chair; the way Patrick had said *woman,* gracious as a man opening the car door, it made Angela a passenger. "You're probably seeing it from a woman's point of view. Maybe that's good. Who knows? I guess it all depends on what judge we get."

"I assure you, I approach a case from a lawyer's point of view."

"Yeah. I'm sure you do," he said mildly.

"Do you have trouble with my being a woman?"

Patrick looked at her hands. Angie looked down; her skin was beautiful, her fingers fleshy but tapered, pointed. "Women are never trouble," said Patrick. She resisted the inclination to put on her jacket.

Her distraction made her seem awkward and childish, artlessness a compelling quality in a body so gauzy and voluptuous. It was one of Angela's most seductive qualities. Sam had identified this for her many years ago; he had assumed he was merely articulating what Angela knew, like he was reading aloud. Since then, Angela's absent moments were shorter and less frequent. She closed her mouth. There was so much, and nothing, to say. Her protest rolled off the glossy surface of Patrick's ambivalence. It was like speaking with Sam.

"I haven't got much time," she said.

"Oh, nothing happened anyway. Police are paid to see things. So when there isn't enough to look at, they look at what's there very carefully. They get anxious. Like they take a piece of information and smash it to see what's inside. Funny when you think about it. Like a monkey with a clock. Then they get all mixed up because the thing they've smashed isn't the thing they had in the first place."

"Yes." He was perhaps the most beautiful man she had ever seen. "Could we get back to that particular afternoon?"

He snapped his fingers. "That's exactly what I mean. Anyway, it's your game. She just started, in a way it's funny, she went back upstairs, you know when they run a movie backwards? She trotted back to her bedroom. I guess, well obviously she had a phone up there and she called the cops. And the fire department. And two rescue trucks. I'd hate to see what would've happened if there'd been a cat up a tree. I call it overkill."

Angela threw her head back and let out three bleating notes, ha ha ha. She could feel her lips and the impulse to mourn. She reserved judgement. Patrick owned the privilege of an unloved space, unconditional indifference. She would get this agreeable man out of trouble. She advised him to say nothing, do nothing, when they went before the judge. His innocence would be explicit. She would speak for him. She rose to shake his hand. He looked like he lifted weights. His skin, his eyes, were perfectly clear, healthy and vital as someone who avoids stimulants. He grinned, a boyish quality that he would likely never lose, and his face was made of alder, the eyes moved in their sockets. He looked at her clothes, her shoes, the cream leather belt. Above them, a camera recorded their ordinary ritual. Their good taste was a conspiracy. She lifted her face, shook back her hair. One day she would make a decision to end this moratorium. She would suddenly age, maybe she would have a child, she wouldn't be a lawyer anymore. She'd have to hurry or it would be too late. Too late for a baby, too late to learn how to judge people again. It must be difficult, Angela thought while she dumbly pressed the down button over and over, to be a pretty man. It must be even more difficult than it is for a woman to be taken seriously. To be given credit for having some depth.

Games

a surveillance more intimate, a scrutiny . . .

He was lying in the dark. Sam was. Angela would see him by the light of his cigarette when she unlocked the front door. The thick wedge from the streetlight showed her as an improbable figure, her briefcase under her arm, its brass fittings cutting her wrist. She nearly dropped it onto the tiled vestibule and Sam pictured the cracked tile and heard the dry clicking sounds of her entry and saw her shadow misshapen by the end of the tile and the beginning of the thick rug, felt her invade the house, corrosive, wind on blue veins in marble.

She was looking up to the bedroom loft, looking right at him. Sam dragged on his cigarette so she could make out his face.

"Sam?"

"Yes honey."

"Why aren't there any lights on?"

"Did you get him off?"

"Who?"

"That good-looking young man. Did you get him off?"

"Yeah. I won. What's the matter with the lights in this place?" Angela was trying the switch by the open front door.

"The power is out."

Angela looked back to the garden, the lamps like large mushrooms lining the path. "But it's not out anywhere else."

"Just at our house I guess Angel. Why don't you come here?"

Angela closed the door. She stood still. There was the sound of ice in a glass. She put her hand to her eyes like someone squinting into the sun. Sam laughed. "What are you doing?"

She laughed too. "How can you see anything? Why didn't you light a candle?"

"I thought you'd like it. Don't you find it romantic?"

"Bloody weird," she said so quietly Sam wondered if he was meant to hear.

"What's that?" He was polite.

"Nothing. I can't see, that's all." Angela sighed. "I'm tired Sam. Do we have to play games tonight?"

Sam was running quickly downstairs. Angela said, "It's all right Sam, I can find a flashlight." Then he was in the kitchen rummaging through a drawer. "Got it." And once again, Sam's location was the only thing she knew in the dark. "Turn it off Sam. Please." She tripped over the edge of something sharp, it cut her shin. Angela touched the cut. "Please Sam, here look, I'll find the candles."

He turned off the flashlight. Angela stood still. Through the window, ashen light, the absence of walls, the sporadic arrangement of furniture in the glass house. She laughed a little. "Watch your step," said Sam.

Angela felt her way to an oriental table. She opened it too fast, she pulled out the drawer. Small ornaments fell from their velvet casings, the clattering of silver trinkets and spoons and brass rings, and a palm-sized crystal globe rolled and shattered into fine splinters at Angela's feet. She was crying then, perhaps a piece of glass had cut her when she ran her hands over the floor seeking the candle, a match.

She lit many candles all over the house, crying loudly, a

bleating noise. She cupped the flame with her cut hand, stepped over the fractured glass to the liquor cabinet, poured a brandy, hesitated, poured one for Sam. At the end of the horseshoe couch Angela dropped off her shoes and curled up, holding her drink in her lap. She cried hard, in the intimacy of a marriage, to lose face, to crumple, to be impersonal.

Sam bandaged her hand. He removed her stained suit jacket. He reached under and pulled her stockings over the cut on her leg. He covered her with a cotton sheet from their bed. All the white candles were burning. Angela had drunk a lot of brandy and she dozed with the thick contentment that comes after such weeping. He held her like she was a little girl; she felt like one.

"And now, Angel, tell me about your day."

"Today? You were there. That was nice of you to come over Sam." She was watching the uneven flames, many liquid flames on the shining table. "Why did you?" she asked then. "I didn't know you were there."

"We don't always know where we are, do we?"

She looked at him then. Her face was swollen and moist, her impossible hair orange in the strange light. "That's not the first time you've done that," she said. "Watched me. When I didn't know you were there."

He wouldn't let her see his eyes. She felt ashamed for him and looked carefully at the reflection of the candlelight on the windows. After a while, in a small sweet voice she asked him, "How was your day?"

His body flinched. It was becoming familiar, this nervous shock running through Sam. He said, "It's OK. You don't have to."

With more hope she pulled away from him, saw that his eyes were calm for a change, calm and the nearly white irises. With a bigger voice she said, "It's nice of you to come and see me in court Sam. Only I'd rather know if you're there."

He covered her with the sheet. "Next time. I'll be the one with the hard-on in the last row."

"It always sounds funny when you talk like one of the boys."

"But you still haven't told me," said Sam.

"Told you what?"

"Did you—get him—off?"

"Patrick?"

"Oh! His name is Patrick is it? Is it Pat or Patrick?"

"I did tell you Sam. I said it when I first came home."

"Oh yes I forgot."

"It wasn't a big deal. He'll get a suspended sentence. Kid made a dumb mistake."

"He's hardly a kid. He's a grown man. And he's very nice looking."

She chose her words carefully. "Yes, he is. He's nice, kind of innocent. Who knows? He's probably quite nice."

"He noticed you."

"He had other things on his mind Sam."

"He did," Sam said. "I could see that with my eyes shut."

Sam seemed very tired. He rested his head on the back of the couch. His face was the calm cleansed face when the mask is removed, the life-lit flesh behind clay. Angela ran her hands on his face like she was bathing him. Her tenderness was forgetful. She had faith in beginnings. This was Angela's gift to Sam, to be forever a novice. She would remember this, when everything else had burst its frame, when she could no longer remember the rules of the game, the punch line or the joke, she would remember to forget everything in their marriage and begin again as if nothing had happened. He was tired. She waited for him to fall asleep, and then she slipped away.

Porsche

Sharon was a mannish woman, built to practise law. Articulate, ironic, canny and handsome, she had great mental and physical vigour. Perhaps it was a natal predisposition. Sharon's single failing had once been an advantage; she had an addiction to nicotine. They sat outside, Angela, Sharon, and Regina, on the steps of the law library. They sat in the sun, scribbled by the wrought-iron shade of the banisters, and told stories while Sharon smoked. Sharon had developed her storytelling techniques through the composition of entertaining and concise factums.

There once was a man who loved a woman more than he loved himself. Now, this man was shy and intellectual and he had once enjoyed a good book and the company of children. It was thought that he would marry a nice girl and settle with a mortgage and a family, she said. *You know. Like Sam.*

She was a selfish but beautiful woman with a taste for athletes and money. But he loved this superficial woman with such intensity, he could do little else. His business began to fail, his health suffered, he drank quantities of whisky and slept on the floor in front of the television.

He began to follow her, although she didn't know it. And the amazing thing is, she was perfectly ordinary in her actions, it would seem, going to and from work, calling him when she said she would call him, shopping and having lunch with friends. But the more ordinary her actions, the more suspicious he became. He couldn't believe that a beautiful woman who loved cheap glamour (I saw her once on the street, nails out to here, the leopard-skin dress, the wolf coat, high heels in winter, kind of gorgeous in a slutty way), he just couldn't get it through his skull, this dame could love a man like him.

The more he loved her, the more he hated himself. And the more he hated himself, the more he distrusted the woman. He tapped her phone. He hired somebody to follow her when he had to go out of town. He couldn't put his finger on it, but he just knew something was going on behind his back. Maybe he was right. We'll never know.

When he was with her, he watched every move she made, and although he was only looking for evidence of infidelity, she thought he was romantic and austere. She'd had a remote father and she thought masculine affection was expressed through disinterested observation. She thought it was sexy, that he studied her without comment, that he wouldn't touch her till she'd made the first move. He was good looking, and the insomnia and mild alcoholism only made him look more rugged and commanding. And besides, he was very, very rich.

But the recession hit him hard, and business got worse and worse. He laid off his staff, sold his buildings, and then one day he woke up on the floor of his repossessed condominium to discover that he owned only one thing. A two-year-old Porsche. Yellow. Bright yellow. A great car.

The man peeled his elegantly ravaged body off the floor. He took a flask of cognac and a hammer, went out to his car, and drove away. This was last fall when we had that great weather.

It was a lovely day. Absolutely no wind, not a breath. The leaves had stayed on the trees all through September. He drove through town and out to the country. There was a road running from the highway to the river. The water was low and it left a wide muddy shore. A few people were fishing. Likely, they envied the man in the Porsche. No one can say how he spent the day. But by all accounts, he arrived at the river at approximately four, and sat all evening, sipping cognac, and watching the people fishing on the other shore.

It had been so warm, we still had mosquitoes. When the sun set, it must have been unbearable, because nearly everyone packed up and left. There was no moon, a very dark night early in October. He thought no one was about. He finished his cognac. He had a flashlight in the glove compartment and by this light he wrote a note for the woman. I hate you, it said, I hate you. Isn't it odd? That he would understand everything just at that moment. Then he took the hammer and began to beat himself. He hit his ribs and chest and arms. He hit his back, his neck, his head. He was somewhat atrophied and thin. But men are so strong. He hit at his head with the blunt end of the hammer. He broke the skull. The Porsche had yellow leather and pale yellow chamois on the roof, soaked with his blood, and the windows were so splattered that when it was discovered, no one could see inside.

Sharon dropped her cigarette and stepped on it. "Hmmm," said Regina, thinking. "Hmmmm." They stood and stretched, yawning and gathering their bags. Angela steadied herself against Sharon while she slipped into her shoes. "I've got so much bloody work to do," Angela said.

"Poor Boopsie." Regina kissed her cheek. "Defender of innocence. Maker of big bucks."

They ambled through the glass doors of the library, and spoke quietly, how it was a sin to be inside on such a summer day. The stairway was like a block of print, blocks of stone and steel, monochromatic, minimal variations on the hypotenuse.

"I'm having Pythagorean hallucinations," said Sharon.

"Oh you wild thing." Regina's hand pinched Sharon's printed buttocks, Sharon silenced and pleased to be the subject of an inappropriate gesture.

The library was noisy, full of law students, their clean intelligent faces triangular, their mind muscles surveying the new boundaries, the drive to exceed. Loudly, they memorized precedence, cooperative and well balanced. The three women had found a table by a window. They worked quietly for an hour and three quarters. Sharon knew it was exactly an hour and three quarters because it was the duration of a longish movie and her body craved a smoke. Regina pushed her Bible-sized addendum away from her, making gagging sounds and pushing her pen down her throat. "Was it hormones?" she asked.

"What hormones?" asked Sharon, fingering her cigarette, the glands under her tongue tightening.

"Male, you know. Male hormones."

Angela was working on the appeal for a heavy sentence for a rape. "Nobody ever talks about that," she said. "I wish they would. I could use it for the defence."

"Whose hormones?" Sharon asked Regina, and she bit upon her cigarette; the way it bit back eased the glottal choke.

"The man's. His time of the month."

They all looked blankly. It must have been the will of the summer sun that inflicted upon Angela a vision of Patrick's pants, his expensive jeans, the tidy and angular way he tucked himself against his thigh. An image terribly innocent and clear, it aroused in her a maternal pulse, an erotic charged with compassion. She scraped back her chair, and looked keenly at the velvet on Regina's lip. "Which one?" she asked.

"The Porsche man."

"A yellow Porsche," said Angela. She was speaking her way into focus. "A great car."

"Hormones? No way. He did it with a hammer."

Regina snorted loudly, a sound similar in pitch to a xerox machine and therefore absorbed into the general ambiance of the law library. Angela felt her molars seized by a small-fisted giggle, it shook her vertebrae like an old woman beating out a carpet, Angela's cheeks pleated, the giggle a permanent crimp in her windpipe. "He did that, self-inflicted. That fantastic car. Ohhh bloo— oh jesus, that's awful. All over the place."

Regina wept when she laughed, wiped at her eyes, "Took a hammer," she wailed, students watching, their silent vows to age gracefully.

Sharon, phlegmatic, wished she could laugh, envied anyone the luxury of hysteria, laughed or tried to, and said, "I know. It really is awful. What a waste of a Porsche."

Vanishing Acts

You could see the ambulance through the mirage of water on the hot streets. Its siren knifed through the thick rind of noon. They sat under umbrellas at The Garden drinking Mexican beer. The waiters wore white shirts with skinny ties and tight black pants, long-waisted, like courtiers in a spa. "Hello," he had said, "my name is Troy, and I will be your waiter this afternoon."

Angela placed pink fingertips on the waiter's sleeve, speaking so low he bent formally. She put her lips to his ear. "We're not ready yet," she said, "thank you."

Regina indicated the curt figure of the departing Troy. "He looks like Sam."

Angela considered it. "Or what Sam thinks he looks like."

"Same nose and same mouth, but the face is wider."

"Sam's wider?"

"Yeah. Sam's wider. Of course he's older. People get wider as they get older," said Regina, summing up. "How is he?"

"Sam?"

"That nervous guy you're married to. How is he?"

"Fine." Angela looked away. "I think I'm falling in love with skin."

"Any skin in particular?"

"Nope. Just skin. All of it." She turned to Regina, touched her cheek lightly. "It looks nice and it holds everything in."

"There's something really weird about you, Desdemona."

They sat quietly, Regina looking at the extreme femininity of Angela's profile.

"How's it going with the rape appeal?" Regina asked.

"Oh I'll get that guy off. Reasonable doubt."

"The old nugget. What, she didn't scream?"

"Nope. It was consensual. Plus, he's Spanish. He hardly knows any English. Says 'eject' for 'ejaculate.' "

"Flimsy."

"She told a wild tale. Beyond belief. You should read my factum. I'm getting better than Sharon."

Their table was beside a fence but through its vertical boards Angela could see the garbage bin. From the bin, the smell of mesquite and garlic, a smell with a taste in it, and the wasps like miniature helicopters patrolled their table. Angela and Regina brushed away the wasps raiding the butter. "Humans should have a tail," said Angela.

"Oh this beer," Regina yawned very wide, "makes me sleepy."

Staring at Regina's blanched tongue, Angela suddenly thought of fish on sand. There was no shade, the sun acute. "Pardon?" She hadn't heard Regina's next remark, another siren and sea gulls complaining. Crows on parade proudly chewed bread crusts.

"I said it's funny how soon we change our ideas about what's sexy." Regina nodded toward the legs of a woman seated nearby. "Remember tans?"

Angela rubbed her own calf beneath the table. "I think it looks nice," she said. "People still tan don't they?" A survey. The colours that year were murky, coagulated with dye, the cotton wrinkled and casual. The Garden was crowded with pale diners, their hands stroking glasses of green beer, and from the shade of their Panama hats they watched themselves in one another's sunglasses. "They look beautiful," said Angela. "They don't look real."

"Their clothes are made on ships in factories that float around the oceans." Troy stood, impassive, at their table. He spoke to the air above them. "They pull up at a dock in the Third World and they load a lot of people who will work in the factories on the ship and then from another country they take on rolls and rolls of fabric and people sew the clothes at sea. That way, there are no countries. And when there are no countries, there are no names. The clothes are very cheap because the people who make them aren't on paper."

His face was bland and informed. Then, pinching his nose tight, he suppressed a sneeze and resumed his pose as if nothing had happened. "And now, ladies," he said, "have you decided to order?" The menu was covered with palm trees.

In her haste, Angela tipped over Regina's beer. "I don't think that's possible," she said. "They can't do that."

"Be nice," Regina said to Angie. "Is it true?" She squinted at Troy, mopping beer.

"You bet. Now what would you like?"

Angela had the sense of a small betrayal to Sam, letting this inaccuracy fly by. It stayed with her, though she seemed lost between pasta and the *charcuterie*. But Regina, drawn by Troy's jiblike nose, needed to know, "Are you always a waiter?"

Troy bowed slightly. "MBA. I do tables when I need the hours."

"You're getting an MBA? At U of M?"

"Ten-four," said Troy. "Have I told you our specials?"

"So what are you going to do? I mean after your MBA?"

Angela smiled as she waded through Light n'Hearty, listening for the toasted belligerence that flavoured Regina's encounters with men.

"Clothing," said Troy. "I'm going into textiles." Regina's smattering of a smile, Troy's insensibility, both cool. Angela had long ago quit trying to mediate. Regina with her blunt brown hair and nice features, a face so regular and discreet people constantly mistook her for Susan, Deb, Barb, for countless tidy women, so they would stop her on the street and hold her arm and ask how she is and begin to ask for Ted or Jim or Bob, and then they'd stop, embarrassed, recognizing in Regina a satiric edge, and they would apologize while Regina smirked at them, all-knowing, and afterwards they would remember her with discomfort and they would hope to see her again, perhaps to set things right. Anyway, Troy, smooth as salt, didn't need help. His eyes focused on the umbrella stand, on the spokes of the umbrella, or a wasp that had settled there while Angela requested the Cajun wings. He didn't write anything down.

Mannequins had been displaced by salesgirls, swivelling their limbs in glass boxes, the music a percussive hula hoop. Angie wrapped her arm around Regina and played with the silk loops of her tweed jacket, blindly dissecting the coloured threads. Like a spectator at a tennis match, her eyes enumerated the girls' differences, one blonde, one brunette, the brunette's hips broader and her movements smaller with greater repetition than the lean geometric postures of the blonde.

The mall was mirrored right through to the carbonated transparencies of Power Works, the aerobics centre. They walked through the courtyard. Regina bought a frozen yogurt at a kiosk. Everyone was tired. A little girl skipped between orange toadstools under the gaze of a pasty-faced man.

There were three young musicians busking in the mall. Their girlfriends were sucking on straws stuck into empty wax cups. Every few minutes one of them would dutifully toss change into the open guitar case. Their jeans were carefully torn. The girlfriends like pink flamingos arranged around three young men, one of them with a cigarette in the side of his mouth, his hair red as Angela's and if you looked closely you would see they were singing. "Shush," said Angela and she put her hand over Regina's lips and then licked yogurt from her own fingers.

"How retro," said Regina, "gratuitous nerd-hippies."

Angela hadn't seen shoulder-length hair on men since law school. The redheaded man folded in half and he twisted a dial on his amp. The muscles of his face contracted, perhaps he remembered a missed errand. He looked at Angela. She screened him for the various reactions: not lust, not admiration, not even curiosity. The guitar player looked at Angela like a salesman looks at a customer, confident, intimate, as if the old music were stolen goods.

Angela's straight blue skirt tucked between her crossed legs, her metronomic toe, in blue, a shiny cotton shoe. Shadows crossed the slate still wet with brown wash from the invisible washerwoman's bucket, then a flock of swallows shadowed Vs across the courtyard.

Angela headed for Power Works. The musician had fixated on her vacant chair. The mouth of the pasty man opened while he watched his dancing daughter. The girlfriends danced too, or they might have been dancing, they moved their little shoes, they moved their lips.

The mirrors were geodesic. Many Angelas swimming through nostalgia thick as seaweed. She hurried, undressing in the mirrored hall. "Hi," they said. "Hey Angie!" Everyone knew her. Through the two-way mirror, the low-impact class cooling off, Angela met the eyes of a woman she knew and she waved but the woman was looking at her own reflection, stretching her calf muscles, the muscle a lozenge, the fluorescent green leg, Angela thought of wintergreen, she swallowed. They were marching and the whip-synth vibrated through Power Works' fragile construction. The beat set off a high-pitched tinny sound, a wolf note. Angela zipped herself into a pink body suit. It had metallic threads so it sparkled when she moved, a cellophane skin.

The room smelled of rubber and sweat. She took deep breaths and focused on the reflective thread on the ridge of her shin. Well-developed thigh muscles made everyone pigeon-toed. Angela's favourite was a perfect woman, tall and thin, her pelvic bone wrapped in a tin-foil leotard with red G-string and bra, like a package of du Maurier.

It was the Advanced Hi-Energy Calorie Buster. Angie always stood behind the du Maurier woman, forcing herself to keep up. When the class ended, she began to black out. The sweat was cold on the back of her neck, and she could feel her own bowels. She sat with her head between her knees, casual, pretending to rest. The class emptied. Then she felt a cold cloth on her neck. She looked up sideways, too sick to lift her head. Regina knelt beside her, lifting her hair from her face. "You've got to slow down, kid," Regina said.

An instructor called in from the doorway, "Time to go, ladies. I've got a class coming in."

Angela pulled away from Regina. "I'm OK," she said.

Sam was scheduled to pick her up outside because they had tickets for the symphony. Late, she ran across the courtyard and she thought she saw Patrick. It was Patrick, for sure, a leather jacket. He was walking away but that waltz-walk was unmistakable. She called, "Hi Patrick!" He waved without turning around. But they had in common their stylish haste, a nice affinity, though she wished he'd seen her. She rushed through the revolving doors. Sam was parked outside. Fitting herself gracefully, tucking in her legs last, filling the car with her perfume, she apologized and kissed Sam's smooth face. He was watching the doors. She glanced back. Patrick walked out, looking at them without recognition. The reflection of the marquee lights made it impossible to see inside. Besides that, Sam had tinted windows. Pressing her hand against the glass, she said, "There's Patrick!" Turning to Sam. "That's the guy!"

Sam pulled away from the curb, driving fast, as he always did. Angela said more casually, "That was that funny guy who walked into the woman's house because the door was open."

"Oh yeah."

She looked back, trying to see Patrick on the crowded street. "It's weird to see him. I'm not used to seeing clients. Randy says he sees his clients all the time on the streets." She settled back. The nausea hadn't quite left. She wouldn't tell Sam. "I never do," she said.

Sam had made all the arrangements. Parking was scarce. Angie had made them late so Sam dropped her to go alone to find a spot. He joined her as the house lights went down. The Schubert was bottom-heavy, the strings slow to get out of bed. It seemed so sewn up, there was no way inside. Angela clutched her own shoulders, her hands full of shoulder-pads. She was very thirsty. The music was exactly like life, she'd try to tell this to Sam later, a maze of repetition and motif, a couple of flimsy ideas made busy. She couldn't remember the last time music had moved her. There was no music anymore, she felt like she'd never heard any.

At intermission a woman in a white full-length rabbit-fur coat, a bikini and stilettos walked around selling next fall's season tickets. Angela needed a drink. Sam worried that it would be too late to get dinner so it was easy to persuade him to leave. Walking out, she placed her feet diagonally to him, taking pleasure in her own long legs; suddenly pleased, she touched his arm. "That music already happened," she said. He smiled at her. There was no one else she could have said that to. She put her arm around his shoulder and swung her legs.

They found a small lacy restaurant with "local catch," and they laughed about that because the only local catch would be whitefish full of mercury, or maybe frogs from Forest Lake Estates. She placed her arms on the table (her breasts under white silk lay on the table too; Sam, watching them, thought of driving into snow), she said, "I feel like I'm on a trip today. I've been walking from one table to another all day long. Except for a workout. One table after another with all these service people bringing me stuff. Thank you," she said and accepted salmon mousse with capers. "See?"

Sam told Angela about his day. His partner in the company was screwing him around. The man's name was Ren. It was a made-up name because Ren's real name was too complicated for American ears. He was Sam's best, or only, friend. When they were first married, Sam had had a network around him, a rolodex of friends. It was one of the things that had made him so attractive. When they travelled, Sam could call up people anywhere; big trade centres like Frankfurt, villages in Peru yielded CEOs or local mayors, men with smiling families eager to cook for them, show them the inside of an exotic life. But lately—for how long?—Sam's contacts had fallen off. He learned that the guy in Frankfurt had stolen $300,000 from the company, that the local mayor was inclined to sleep with young girls. Sam would come home in a rage when he learned about this, and he and Angie would go out that night, glad to have each other. Sam was an idealist. His friend in Frankfurt had reminded him that $300,000 was less than two percent of the company's tax evasions. And the mayor of Callao said that the girls were supporting their families on their earnings, and besides that, said the mayor licking his cigar, they liked it. Sam had told these stories to Angela and they became currency at their dinner parties, which were increasingly dominated by Angela's friends, especially the women, Sharon and Regina. Angie's friends adored Sam. They laughed, elated, sympathetic, when Sam brought fresh evidence of the world's betrayal. They would jump up from the table and walk around to put their arms on his chest from behind and bend over him, their hair touching his cheek, laughing tenderly, "Poor Sam! That's awful!" They delighted in the salacious details of a recent scam, but Angela would watch the wound open on Sam's face and she felt something inside herself retreat every time Sam would use his new expression, "Honest to god, it makes me sick, these people should be in jail." And gradually the world slipped away from Sam's ideals and robbed old ladies in the back lane. And eventually, only Sam and Angie were left walking the high road without a map. It had happened so slowly, Angela felt they'd always lived in a small place, always treading a thin line in the dark.

Sam was worried that Ren had been fraudulent in a Hong Kong contract. He was working around what he called "the central fact," which was an event that had occurred two months earlier, a letter that never arrived, and when Sam had called, Ren wasn't at the hotel, maybe he wasn't in Hong Kong and if he wasn't in Hong Kong then where was he? Angela offered several explanations, but this strategy backfired because the variety of her explanations proved Sam's point; anything might have happened, his partner was clearly out of control. "You need to define the problem," she advised him. "Make a list of questions and ask Ren direct, face to face when he gets back."

"I have all the questions already. I just don't have any answers," said Sam.

She had become immune to Sam's troubles. It was a credo in her faith in their marriage: the world didn't matter very much; they would survive. Angela ate joyfully, her mouth full of wine and butter and her mind become her lawyer's mind listening to Sam's suspicions. This was travel too, from Sam's wife to Sam's lawyer; easier to attend to Sam when reason and technicalities were the succour. But Sam was a difficult client. She loved the lines that ran from his nose to the side of his mouth and the neat lines tucked into the tissue under his eyes. She touched his face, Sam's skin, the emollient of his charm. Her hand went right through him, as if she would never actually touch him. Their conversation died.

She ordered cake, a strawberry torte she loved, and was devouring it, leaning one arm on the table and absorbed in dumb pleasure. They would appear to be a complacent married couple, frankly greedy and uncompelled by the lull in the conversation. She forked neatly the last pink icing. And looked up. "You're not having any?" she asked Sam. She put down her fork. The self-loathing was familiar, evoked childhood. Caught in an action unconscious and meanly gratifying.

"You were hungry," Sam said.

"Must have been all that shopping." She looked down at her scraped plate. "I don't know what got into me."

"Cake," said Sam.

"Sam, I think, I really think I want to have a child."

He looked at her with regret, as someone who is hearing a confession from a pathological liar, with love and sad compassion.

They had brandy. Angela the lawyer was too drunk to prevent Angela the wife from becoming maudlin. They argued about whether Angela had enjoyed Hawaii more than Vermont. Sam remained lucid. He observed that Angie contradicted herself on several points. When he asked for a good cigar, she took it from him and inhaled it deeply and threw up on the way home.

Light

Since his partner had vanished, Sam had been floating on an aftermath like a convection current strong enough to sustain his glide indefinitely. Until he knew the extent of Ren's betrayal, Sam couldn't act upon the fresh leads coming into their office. There was plenty to do in servicing their existing clients, but he couldn't focus. His work had become unmetred and he learned the pain that comes with an absence of rhythm, the air bruised by the incongruous alliance of one minute with another. Everything was flushed to the surface, as if a bomb had exploded underwater. There was no understanding the rain-dust on glass, an inaccurate billing, the laughter of children heard suddenly through his window at a red light, a black shirt thrown on a chair, his wife's sad eyes, e-mail from Taiwan, the size of the *New York Times,* the surprising familiarity of his own hands, trade talks in Geneva, mould on the fridge door, not days but particles, bits, spasms of information, light without mind. When a jet flew overhead it made waves in his veins.

His office was located in the heart of downtown. It was a

rare object in a prairie city. Four storeys high with an elevator, a black box oiling up and down the shining yellow exterior. The building looked like a bee, like an industrial insect. Inside, the ceilings were high, traversed by aluminum beams and black extrusions. Its walls were covered by very large paintings of the kind only corporations can afford to purchase. Windowless, the single piece of glass was in a skylight like a matrix at the centre of a hole which ascended through all four storeys to a convex rose window on a flat roof. Sam worked on the fourth floor just off-centre from the rose window in a large space purified by filters and humidifiers, an area determined more by light than by walls. The leaded glass sent spectrums through the air.

It was, again, Sunday. Before Ren had failed him, the days had been firmly made and distinguishable. But now, one day leaked into the next, Tuesdays with the excitable complexion of a Friday, or a Thursday that wasn't any day at all. It would have been better had there been sorrow, a softening of effect, humane sorrow like a walk on dry grass when the sun is diffused and warm. Sam regretted the breathing days when he could yet walk on the bottom of his heart, before he had emigrated to the larger space of his unfixed despair. Sometimes on a Sunday when the old patterns of difference and rest were most haunted and absent, when the healthful world played catch and opened car doors for elderly mothers, when the streets were full of the fluorescent cross on the cyclists' orange jackets and their tonsured helmets, on a Sunday his panic, like unearthly cold, cracked his nerves and the room would fold with a fast sedimentary flow, a rippling seizure. Everywhere, Sam would think, it is the same.

His tubular black desk had been inspired by Bertolucci's film *The Conformist*. He had bought the desk ardently in love with gun-beauty. Sam was protective of his desire for design. He was talented in the ways of irony, weariness, distraction, indifference, and hedonism. He sheltered his talents as one would shelter lovemaking from our view. He would never look directly at this aspect of himself, his feminine appetite for expensive style. It was something he did by proxy and perhaps not for his own advantage. Because everyone expected him to live up to a finished exterior, it was their weakness Sam humoured, for their sake. Him, it left weary. And in the stark anachronic day, like a cheated investor, Sam learned that a certain anger helped; rage like a sentry, an ironic watcher at pain's threshold. He had always been strong. We must do what we must do. But the loneliness, it must feed his anger too.

It was a windy day. Clouds staved the sun passing through Sam's office and the paper on his desk was alternating pink or grey; the effect of both and their enharmonic scales exhausted him. The importer, his own porous breed, was effectively extinct. It was necessary to pretend he didn't know this, to continue working, like a scribe in a computer shop. These days, everybody wants to skip the middleman and buy direct. One of his best customers, a low-end clothing retailer, had finally discovered the fax machine, cancelled Sam's agent in the Orient, and ordered directly from the factory. The account had been his company's largest source of revenue; their velour track suits made steady sales in a market so stable it seemed bovine. The product was cheap at its source and affordable at its destination, and somewhere in between, Sam's company agitated the process like heating molecules so they will move quickly and expand. Everything is made in China. With the fidelity of a man who will love an unfaithful woman, Sam had a skill for naming integrity into imported products. *Country of origin,* like a powerful myth, became the place where the buttons were done up, though the fabric was manufactured in China, dyed in Korea, assembled in Hong Kong according to designs stolen from France and revamped for snowbirds in Florida. The validating *country of origin* was a kiss for sale. It was a mistake to underestimate the usefulness of the importer.

And now Ren, his best partner, had disappeared into a digital lapse in Sam's analogic imagination. Ren was a Japanese Canadian educated in Switzerland, small, cheerful, impeccable. Spoke seven or eight languages, he said, depending on how much wine he'd drunk. A black belt, an expert skier who preferred heli-skiing, a pilot, a bachelor, Ren could take over any argument with international comparisons so large in scope he baffled his competitors, their chests would sag, lose that aggressive thrust, they would suddenly sit back and the confident ones would ask Ren questions, making subtle requests for a piece of the action, while the older men with grey pouches beneath their eyes got away from the table as soon as possible and told each other while they gave themselves a shake, zipping, that the guy was full of shit, another one of these cons taking over.

In a high smooth voice, Ren released into trains, jets, dining rooms around the world his quickly uttered stories of international trade. Sam always thought of him as defined by his gold Rolex. Ren was lithe, even in his mid-thirties; it made the rest of the world seem bland and conventional. Sam felt excited and released in Ren's company. Life was sharply detailed, quick, and the younger man's ambition woke Sam up. They were blunt without being confessional. It was clean, clear-headed, Sam called it "professional." Sam's domineering style passed through the buoyant agent without altering in any way Ren's hermetic cachet. Sam's power came from his intimate knowledge of the markets, Ren's from his mercurial detachment. Sam was homed and tightly located; Ren was cosmopolitan and lived lightly in cyberspace.

But it was Sunday, and Sam was alone. Once he'd felt he created and controlled the seductive interior. Steel filing cabinets of the kind gallery owners use to store paintings, sliding silently out, deceptively slender, holding his history, the route he'd taken that had seemed like progress. Freedom is the only thing we want. There was a time when this room with its explicit and casual wealth was an expression of his capacity to control and to create. The silent spare linearity of his office, erotic as money will be, was not merely luxurious: Sam had made it, it was occupied by his employees, he worked with complete, unfettered efficiency.

But it was Sunday. And Ren had vanished. The crisis in revenue caused by the lost textile account shouldn't be critical, should be slept away by the hypnotic will. Sam didn't believe in hindrances. He wasn't superstitious. He wouldn't be trapped by velleities on the quick ascent, the fast track. His heart was idling high. He took off his jacket, unbuttoned his shirt, Sam, elegant at his visible core. As Angela would say, he looks well-dressed naked.

Pacing (he would not call it aimless), he checked his fax for a message from Ren, and met Ren's absence, the agent's most successful joke. Sam swung his left arm and walked and breathed. He was sorry to lose Ren's talents, worried over Ren absconding with e-files, and jealous of the man's escape, to slip away, to change one's number. It was imperative to locate him. Sam's territory was radically curtailed by Ren's exit; there had never before been a frame around him, a whispering border. It brought to mind the ambivalent quality of Sam's freedom. Its transparency, the hesitant hour, how his arm detached itself from him and though his blood was in stasis, the pulse in that arm was fast, very fast, he was only glad he wasn't being watched when by separate volition the arm rose in the air, trembled, stayed. Pale, waxy, his body produced a nervous sweat; unlike the athletic scent he would achieve playing tennis, this was a shameful smell. His paralysis lasted long enough for him to name it; as soon as he called the word forward, it was over. He could move. He took his chair. He looked straight ahead. He waited indefinitely for Angie to call him home.

Marlene

Joey grew up on a farm till he was six. All he could remember was a horse named Blue because she was, in her winter coat, quite blue. And later in summer Blue was grazing in the flax, blue for a little while every summer that Joey could remember being on the farm with his mother and father and a baby brother before the fire wiped everything out including much of Joey's memory, though he still, Angela discovered, remembered Blue.

The family had been sleeping when the fire broke out. When Joey jumped out the second-storey window he broke his pelvis and it didn't heal right. It affected his growth, made him shorter than would be indicated by the size of his hands and feet and his head. He was sent to a foster home. His native blood, obscured by a Ukrainian grandfather, was sufficient evidence of Joey's insignificance. Child and Family Services placed him with a family who accepted many foster children and they were too busy to see the emotional bruises or the hemorrhaging of Joey's capacity to remember anything that wasn't stapled to his skin. The night his parents and little brother burned to death was the last time Joey would understand anything softer than a scream, more delicate than a razor.

A match flamed in the sunlight. A cigarette was like her car; she got a kick out of fashionable vices. She drove with the butt stuck between her lips and when she accelerated, she inhaled deeply, blinking. A good car and a cigarette made her feel muscular, manly, in control. She was devoted to her habits and practised them daily. In her loyalty to the present it was as if she were constantly adjusting the lens, ignoring anything that might distract her from pleasure. This was her obedient sensuality and it made her, Sam said, the kind of woman that men want to marry. She asked what he meant by that. He said that men would be tricked into thinking she'll be just as enthusiastic about their comforts. They'll think she'll protect them from pain.

The car phone was yet another addiction. Sam had wanted her to install it. He told her he missed her when she would spend so much time alone driving (as she liked to do, she would drive and smoke and listen to music with sad, perceptive lyrics and she'd sing and watch the smooth scenery). At first it felt like too many guests at a party. But Sam had appealed to her bad conscience and good manners, suggesting that clients needed to have greater access and her husband simply needed her. She hated to be called selfish. Before long, the phone was louder when it didn't ring and soon she couldn't live without it. It improved her productivity. All the contact she would have missed, acres of silence that now were fully developed, a vacant part of her existence, inhabited. It made her more consistent.

It was the anniversary of her father's death. Every summer she and May would remember him with a quick downward glance. They'd all been caught, deer in the headlights, in automatic motion. They had been a cool, seemingly permissive family. Her father watched May's career with tolerance based on disbelief. His money supported her. May found other people to play the leisurely game of Art. She was in truth a vain woman who brought relief to people who couldn't accept reality, a bit of a barmaid but not so well paid. They had developed an ency-clopedia of alternative subjects and could enjoy many weekends together by virtue of deferral, substitution and, after a couple of drinks, only slightly cruel *double entendre.*

He died fast, over an interval of ten days. Ten days of sus-tained wonder. Sickness so virulent was out of time, something from an older world. Angela felt somehow lightened by the ferocity of this illness. She grieved for him. But it was, in a strange way, a relief to discover an edge, beyond the control of doctors and medicine. His death was surprisingly simple. She hadn't expected it to be healthful, so full of vitality. He had been a brittle man, but when he was very ill, emaciated, lying in the dark with Angie in a chair beside him, he had a humility, new and unencumbered. She stayed with him till he died. He told her it was fine. And she believed this to be true. He wasn't reli-gious. It was the limits of his self that he adhered to, that refreshed him at the end.

But it was her sole encounter with an irrevocable loss. His absence was definite. Everything else was open to interpreta-tion. Her father was gone. She knew now, people can go miss-ing. That they do not come back. Her mother had claimed a sisterly kinship with Angela. She was no one's daughter now. She was surprised, when she looked into mirrors, at how young she appeared. Her father was dead. She ached for a reversal of this fact.

Her parents' marriage had been a truce. The family was lucky and elegant. They were above analysis. For a brief period after his death, she and May were shy with each other. And then the repartee resumed.

The droll, private aspects of May had flourished since he died. She spoke of him with increasing discernment, with fresh objectivity and a lightness like the skill of her once-deft hands, more told in a glance that touched all surfaces with gai-ety, not unkind, unbeseeching. "My husband never did like my paintings," she told a friend at a dinner party. "In fact, he did-n't like me at all!" And she laughed with such joy that her astonished guest laughed with her, grateful for the illusion that this was really funny. It was evident she loved him. And now he was gone, like a habit she'd overcome. That might have been the difference between Angela and May: Angela's marriage made her habitual, while May was increasingly impulsive. They shared their secret journal-writing, though. Sam teased them about it.

Angela was driving. She phoned her mother. "Describe the countryside, darling. I'd like a vicarious thrill. I'm a mother after all." Angela looked out on the hot silky fields. A lark spilled its short song through her window. "I see an owl." The strong hands at the edge of his wings, assurance, shoulders on a bird. "Everything is green."

"I've got something to tell you, Angel. The grass is really red. We have been concealing this from you. But I feel you're ready for the truth."

Stop sign at railway tracks, gravel-dust clouding the car, settling on the dash. Angela loved the feel of dust on her skin in the heat. The world was green and blue. She thought of May, a slice of lemon, yellow dahlias. "I guess I'll never know if I'm seeing the same as anybody else."

"We are over-sensitive about your vision," May told her. "Your father was right, of course, always and inevitably. It is an act of divine retribution. Your defect is my punishment. I am unnatural. I understand that now and I enjoy your handicap."

"Have you looked into this gene-wise, Mum? I expect there's a rational explanation."

"No!" May laughed. "Isn't that typical of me? No, I prefer to live on the edge of your dad's mad myth. It gives me something to reject, and how could I live without that?"

Heat made Angela want to make love. "I want to have a baby, next spring. I could take maternity leave for the summer and be back to work by fall."

"Hell, have it at the office! Just shut the door and cancel incoming calls."

"You don't think I can have a baby and a career."

"I don't think anything of the kind." The closest May ever came to an expression of pain was the rare failure of wit.

Angela couldn't bear the intimacy of her mother's pain. "Weird to be having this conversation now," she said. "I mean we sound like the fifties."

"You married your dad."

"What?"

"I said, I would be glad."

"You said I married Dad."

"Sam is much taller and he's aging better."

"Sam's not at all like him. I get to do whatever I want. Sam likes it that I work hard."

"It's not my business."

"I want a baby. You think it'd be nuts?"

"A baby isn't easy for women like us."

"We're not that much alike."

"No."

Angela switched hands and wiped her palm on her skirt. "Anyway, what's wrong with us, May?"

Her mother's sharp laugh. "Nothing. We're perfect."

Angela's will was in spasm. She thought about watering the plants on the deck; this evening she would catch up on chores like that. It felt like boredom. She wanted to be alone. May caught it like a virus and said, "Anyway Angela, thanks for calling," and disconnected.

With the phone dead in her hand, her jaw stiff with anger, the car coasted to the shoulder, quiet as a boat under sail.

There are always birds. The sun, thick in her lap, a hot thick hand lying on her left arm. She sat with the telephone cradled, her fingers running through the numbers she might call. She was full of a listening, between her fingers and her thighs, up and down, a stem of listening. At a right angle, the highway sounded like wind. The gravel road she travelled, grasshoppers, crickets, the swelling songs. And Angela, listening.

Then she called Patrick. And hung up before anyone answered.

In the crests and troughs of this silence, when the telephone rang, in the seconds before speaking, she wished for Patrick, the way a woman might thirst for an attractive bottle.

Slow to speak into the receiver, slow to disclose her own low and private oscillations, the luxury of silence before making herself known.

Randy always worked Saturdays. Since he'd joined the firm, he'd started working Sundays too. He had to get a base, he needed billable hours badly. He asked her to come down.

"Well I can't," she told him. "I'm going out for dinner with Sam."

Randy's distress somehow erased the play on the line. She pictured him, his weekend clothes, a polo shirt, too small, brand new, bright blue, chewing gum and smoking, in the relaxed off-time that was almost as busy as a weekday on the twenty-seventh floor. She felt truant and yearned to be home. She waited for Randy to say something funny. Randy asked her if she remembered Marlene Cook.

"Sort of. A vamp. Good lawyer. Tough."

Randy told her that Marlene Cook was dead. Angela, seared by anxiety.

"She's not that old," she said.

"Forty-nine."

Stroke, heart attack, suicide, maybe fast-acting cancer, something old-fashioned, meningitis, or AIDS from a blood transfusion in 1983, something mysterious or ripe with possibilities for litigation. Marlene had been a private woman.

"That's awful. Was she a friend of yours?"

She was, apparently. Randy was breathing through his nose.

"Sorry, Randy. I didn't know you guys were friends."

"We're not. She didn't like me. They want somebody from the firm. You've got to get down here," he said. "I can't touch it. It's too fucking creepy. They charged a kid with murder. A kid did it. Fifteen. A boy. Native kid." She could hear Randy light a cigarette. "I don't know why I'm so weirded out. They asked for us. I don't want to talk about it over the phone."

Angela reluctant as a horse turned away from the barn. "Why not over the phone?"

"You're on your cellular, right?"

"Yeah. It's nice here, too."

"You know these things can be tapped. Get in here, will you Angie?"

Melodrama, grief, in poor taste. Still, a murder. It'd been about two years since she'd had one. She should test herself. No choice. Got to go for it. She'd call Sam.

She stopped for ice cream, an antidepressant, and ate secretly, stalling. She was full of windows today and it was dangerous to open any of them or to look out. Her body was at war with itself. She would be vigilant; she would smother her own anarchy. And then, returning to the car, the smell of exhaust. Angela resisting the despair that would make her inhospitable to Randy, make her unprofessional.

Sam answered so fast she didn't think it had rung. "Yes?" he said. His voice was strangely high, like Ren's.

"Sam?"

"Yes?" Again, strange urgency. Did he recognize his wife's voice?

"It's Angela."

"Oh?"

"Didn't you know it was me?"

"Oh shut up," he said, and his Ren-voice rippled. "Of course it's you. Who would it be? Patrick?"

She was going to speak, stopped, a chip of word lodged itself between them.

"Hello?" he said, and hung up as if no one had been there.

Drunk with anger, she called him back. "What's going on?"

"You tell me."

"I'm going to work."

"I know."

"Then I'll be home."

"Well, you still live here."

"Then you're taking me out for dinner."

Sam didn't say anything. She could feel him soften.

"Then," she said, "I'm going to kiss you and we're going to—"

She said "talk" and he said "eat." They agreed.

Feeling better, Angela told Sam about the boy who had been

charged with murder. "Remember Marlene Cook?" she asked him.

When Sam didn't remember someone, it was as if they were discharged from the human race. "No. Don't know her."

"But she's dead."

"Guess I won't get the chance now."

It was unlike him. She felt the line narrow. "Sam? I really love you," she told him. He said he knew that.

"So you're going to the office, are you?" he said.

"I'll finish quick. Randy's in bad shape." It wasn't quite true. She worked harder. "Marlene was a friend of his. Randy seems a bit weirded out."

"That's Randy."

"I love you."

"Yup."

She repeated in her mind, driving the half-hour into town, repeated the conversation, repeated it. She really was going to the office to meet with Randy first and then maybe she'd go to the Remand Centre to interview a new client, a boy charged with murder. Sam's scepticism provoked a circularity in Angela's defence, a weary rondo.

Joey had a hearing problem. He wasn't clinically deaf, but he couldn't hear anything the first time it was said, he was receptive only to the replay. His case workers were familiar with this and said everything twice.

He was asleep sitting up when Angela met him in an interview room. He smelled of dust and mouldy white bread. He wasn't fifteen, he was fourteen. But in addition to mould and white bread and beer, Joey exuded strongly a masculine smell. Sam didn't. Sam smelled of onion and whisky, cigarettes and chocolate. But other men had what could only be defined as a male scent, quite independent of cleanliness. His innocent posture, face disclosed to his unconscious, his large head cantilevered by his dirty hand, and the small body, growth potential energy or growth diverted by the accident of his fall, his parents' death. She spoke his name twice. And of course he awoke for the facsimile.

It was a room diminished by a two-way mirror and the video camera in a corner bracket. The sounds of a tape machine, a surreptitious pulse. Angela was thirsty. A jug of water on the table. She saw herself, as if through the camera, pour a glass of water, drink it, pour a second glass and offer it to Joey and when Joey drank it Angela felt that she had somehow touched him with her lips. The film would be black and white with a long focus; how far away they would look, within the little room. The boy's presence filled Angela with an unbearable nostalgia for Sam. She thought of her father. She would be good to Sam.

Joey had a thickness about the bridge of the nose. His black eyes were frightened, as if he had forgotten how he had arrived. There was no daylight. The window led to another room, much like this one but its opposite, as the relation between exposed and expositor. How could they know what time it was? She looked at her watch. It was three o'clock. It was perhaps three o'clock in the morning. She saw herself at a window that looked outside, snow and the charcoal branches, snow floating thickly in pearl-coloured air, but where would winter be and in what forest? The water tasted flat, she yearned for aerated water. Joey's black eyes were familiar. She was sure she had invented him, this boy, he had come from her in anticipation.

Angela knew him instinctively. She knew, for instance, that she mustn't say anything. She would have liked to stroke his head to caress the thick latency between his eyes and soothe him. He glanced about the room and she thought it must be from a fear of space though the room was small. His terror gradually subsided. At the end of their unhurried hour she had acquired very little of the barrister's information but she was familiar with his wayward presence and she felt that he knew her this way too.

The notepad before her was bright as if it sat in the sun. Joey and Angela gazed at it, their eyes contracted. Their breathing was hypnotic and after a time it overwhelmed Joey who put his head down on the table and fell asleep. Angela motioned to the guard to retrieve the sleeping boy while she filled her arms with paper. Gibbous, she stood a long time in the empty room, her body rocking, and the guard who remained in the observation room looked away from the unspoken confessions running through the muscles of her face.

Secrets

Angela and Mike Souster were walking out by Stonewall, down a quiet road that ran high and black through farmland. From a distance Angie looked like a bit of pink cellophane blown from the city. Up close her dusty skin seemed over-sweet as the roadside roses, her wild hair the colour of the cranberry and dogwood shrubs, yet she retained a synthetic quality. She had never aspired to be entirely natural.

The day was hot but a fresh wind took their words out to the gingham fields. Theirs was a conversation trespassing the boundaries of jurisprudence. Mike was a forensic pathologist and his hands were translucent and white. He walked in city loafers, kicking up fine talc, peering out from a chalky face at the mysteries of farm life. Angela felt their words distributed like dandelions in the broad wind.

Mike told her about the autopsy. He had a high-pitched nasal voice squeezed out of a long neck. Angela asked him to start at the beginning. They couldn't agree as to what the beginning would be. Mike said he always began with the description of the corpse as it was first brought to the lab. Angela wanted him to talk about Marlene: who she was before she'd become a dead body, what kind of work she'd enjoyed, whether she'd had children. She was hungry for news, felt the keen attention she would give to an Amnesty International report.

He was a prudish gossip. Marlene had been a lawyer married to a wealthy guy, some kind of paper money, stocks or securities. She was forty-seven and childless. "She was beautiful," said Angela. "I didn't know she never had any kids." Angela knew her at various functions around town but Marlene had been ten years ahead of her in law school and they'd never crossed professional paths. Angela enjoyed her own drowsy equation of professional paths with this bucolic (illicit) promenade with the pathologist. Mike disapproved of Marlene's resurrection. Angela's words bounced off him like offensive little darts. She confided to him that she'd always felt close to Marlene. "I mean, I didn't really know her but I felt like she'd been there before me. Sort of a pioneer." Then she laughed far too loud, what a gaff, *pioneer*, ex*cuse* the French. Of course Angela might yet have a baby, it wasn't entirely out of the question. Mike stopped and took off his suit jacket, folding it carefully. He wore a dark suit, and his shirt was wet under the arms.

He was more forthcoming after Angela finally permitted him to dispense with Marlene the woman and describe his own interaction with Marlene the homicide.

"She was a mess when they brought her in," he said. Angela stumbled over waves of mud, bumping against Mike like a chum and laughing nervously. "So you tidied her up, eh Mike?"

Mike stopped. The road had climbed a mild incline and permitted them a view of the section across the road. Cattle were rare in those parts; most people planted grain. But there was a beef ranch on the other side. Mike watched the cows. His head tilted to one side, intelligent brown eyes beneath a neat shelf of eyebrows. "Those are cows Mike."

Mike said, "I grew up on a farm. Till I was eight." He turned his focus to Angela. (Angela. Cow.) He said, "Forgot they look like that."

"So anyway," and he lit a cigarette, "she was a mess." Mike walked like a blind man in an empty room, smoking. "It was a normal female body, no congenital malformations. Before she was identified, I estimated the age between thirty-eight and forty-five. It was in healthy condition. There were superficial wounds to the face and much of the body. Bruises, surface abrasions. Lividity in the right abdomen." Angela asked him if she'd been beaten to death. "Well, the larynx and vocal cords were ruptured. Vertebrae crushed at the back of the neck. Prints on the throat area. The skull at the right temple was fractured and there were bone fragments lodged in the brain. Ruptures and occlusion in the right eye would indicate a sharp blow with a blunt instrument. Of course the liver hemorrhaged, that might've done it anyway."

Mike blew smoke. "I could send you my report. She's all there."

"Not exactly."

Angela remembered her from the back; she'd watched her at a fundraising dinner. Marlene had blonde hair worn long and straight and tied at the nape of her neck. She'd been wearing a backless dress and Angela had watched her, fascinated by the shapely spine and the cheekbones when Marlene turned her head to speak to the man beside her. Marlene had a reputation for being ruthless and unapologetic. But Angie hadn't known she never had children.

She had no faith in her own questions then. "Were there any indications of sexual assault?"

"Vaginal trauma. Yes. Severe trauma. Yeah."

The afternoon was ample and overripe. She couldn't think beyond the ticking heat. Angela traced the paths of imaginary horses in the ditches, searching for wire, glass, gopher holes. The culverts were dry. But land so identical yields subtle differences. The fields shimmered like water. Thirsty, she asked about the timing.

"Just speculation," said Mike. "But I'd say she was strangled while he raped her."

They had been walking for an hour and it was much like

standing still or walking on the spot, magnified under the sun's lens and the summer ridge of high pressure, the blue sky pinning them, clearly. Miles of the same, thumbprints on green wheat, cirrus feathers to the south, the eventual cyclonic spin. One red willow break locating them; without comment, they turned there and retraced. She was careful not to touch him, for his sake. She wondered what Sam would think. She wondered if she'd tell him.

Mike seemed a wary and formal man. She unlocked his door. Driving back, Angela felt responsible for his silence. She couldn't remember the things that would normally interest her. The light had failed, leaving the dry countryside stricken and sallow. She was overcome by timidity, afraid to release herself from Mike's estranged company. "Are you all right?" she asked. He looked surprised, nodded, affirmative. She would have liked to turn on the radio but she couldn't acquire the further responsibility for unsatisfying music. What if there were a British symphony? Brass march, or fanfare, an anthem. Had she ever enjoyed music? Catkins, tree frogs, symbols of promise, objects of wonder. She couldn't recall. She looked sideways at Mike, his vellum exterior.

"How's—your wife? Sorry. It's Val isn't it?"

"Val's fine." Mike sat back, relieved, identified, Val's husband. It was inexcusable, but Angela's metabolism was perhaps responding to the anemic landscape. It affected her will, brought forth familiar demons, a mean descent, the fallen daydreams. She imagined Val and Mike making love. Only she was Val. Sam would make himself Mike. Mike kissing Sam. What the mind will do. The highway ran into industrial park. Small beige buildings fronted by parking lots. Employees. Fresh-oiled road. The back tires spit up creosote, a petroleum smell, a fraternal twinning with the copper scent of death which lingered from Mike's reportage of the autopsy. Angela felt queasy. She remembered this. Some forms of pornography made her sick: photographs of the ovens at Auschwitz, a photograph of a soldier with his arm blown off. First viewings of twentieth-century history, at puberty, somehow connected with her initial understandings of sex. Not a promising start, as Sam had said when she confessed this to him. Angela had since learned many versions of power. How to measure blood loss, identify secretions, the post-mortem. Secret side of things. Sam disliked the subject, he felt a horror of her, the edge of that, she never brought it again to light. Something her imagination did despite her. Mike had a thinly fleshed head. Long fingers. Angela pictured the rest of him, a thin pale man without fat, flesh of fish, the body's perfection.

Fidelity

a surveillance more intimate, a scrutiny called love

Of course he was looking into the lens. It was the Mona Lisa effect; his eyes followed hers, everywhere. That was why Angela kept his photograph on her desk where she could watch him while he watched her. At least, she would think in the early morning before the coffee kicked in, before the phone solved the puzzle of loneliness, before her own optimistic blood warmed in a daylight still blue with dreaming, before all this could occur, she would think their mutual surveillance might be an embrace firm and stable. So she kept him in sight while she tried to work.

And Sam stayed, like a white sun at the back of her mind, while Angela read the police report on Marlene Cook's murder.

The cops had taken such professional notes. Details, discrete, quantum, a never-ending demolition of the central event, splintered frames, rags and threads and a splatter of blood, sperm, hair, fingernails, swept and analyzed and tabulated, the scrawled ballpoint respoken into court, the neutral auditorium, an over-punctuated story smashed beyond recognition. The switch for the back porch was on but the light itself was off and this would indicate that either the bulb was burnt out or the switch was dysfunctional. The aluminum easing to the kitchen window which was accessible from the same porch showed signs of recent tampering. Recent tampering? Angela looked up into Sam's fast-film eyes, the portrayal of depth on its shining surface. See Sam? I'm only wondering: how did the cop know the tampering was recent?

She answered the phone.

"Angela." His voice with the boyish swing in it. "Is that you?"

"Yes." Angela kept the professional muscle in her voice. "Who's this?"

"It's me," and the laugh that stayed in his throat, a boy's laugh, it skipped out. "Patrick."

She sat up. "The trespass man," she said.

"What are you doing?"

"I was working. Are you in trouble?"

His laughter was affectionate and casual, a congenial giggle. "No no. Are *you* in trouble?"

The bedroom-office was hot, the heat licking her.

"Of course I am," she said. She leaned back in her chair, lifted an ankle through air suddenly purple. She sighed. It was eleven o'clock. On the foot there is a pocket of flesh formed by the talus and the tibia, much like the oyster-cut under roasted chicken or the cheeks of pickerel, pale and succulent. "We're all in trouble," she said.

He moaned then. "Ain't that god's truth, woman," he said.

Angela draped a hand to the floor, ran it in the dust ribboned through the grooves between the sweating pine planks. "What's up?"

"Nothing. I just want to thank you."

"No problem."

"So if I ever need a lawyer, I'll keep you in mind."

"I'm your man," said Angie.

"Well I might, some day. Not criminal stuff. Maybe buy a business. You do that kind of thing?"

"Sure."

Then he didn't say anything. Very slowly, not making a sound, Angela took her legs from the desk, sat straight and listened. The phone was alive in her hand; Patrick's abrupt reticence, granular and static.

"Just make an appointment," she said at last.

"I'll do that. That's good. Kind of woman you make an appointment with if you want to see her. You're good."

So they said goodbye, several times, take care of yourself, said Patrick, and hung up. Angela hearing how the grackles occupied the mountain ash, suddenly aching and lonely. Take care, take care of yourself. She thought of calling him back. My god what a complete idiot, Angela said, and she shoved on shoes and went out.

She drove with her left leg under her, listening to the radio, trumpet and swing, a couple of miles to the plaza where you could find a dry cleaner and a liquor store and a grocery store with fresh fish on snow where she bought two whole sole because they looked pure as ice though she knew too well how bony sole could be and she bought artichokes and she picked up Sam's shirts and her own dresses. Bob the man who runs the place admired Angela as a dutiful but sexy wife, a happy combination she, giving Bob a smile and she lifted their fabrics so Bob could tie the plastic in a bow at the bottom. Goodbye she said, Bye Bob, and he liked that, it was good to run an operation in a classy neighbourhood and anybody who thinks rich dames are bitchy by definition don't know dick about what money really does for the human spirit not to mention the human physique, complexion, and smell.

Five acres of parking lot bloomed with steaming and polychromatic hatchbacks. Now and then a dog would occupy the driver's seat drooling thoughtfully over the defrost elements, barking, barking, nervous, neutered, pedigree, pets. Angela with her arms full of groceries and dry-cleaning and liquor bumped mazily a path through the vast lot, shimmering and hazy but placid as the seeded fields around a solitary farmhouse. She was chewing gum and the song in her head and the rubato ticktock of her left sling-back shoe distinct from the right, threading the little Japanese cars to the easy mark of her splendid Thunderbird. They were cheap sunglasses sliding on Angela's freckled nose because she was always losing her good ones and they forever break anyway. Inexpensive lenses have that flattening colour-blind effect, whereas Patrick was wearing Vuarnets. He was leaning on the driver's door, his arms folded across his chest, and Angela was unlocking the trunk before she peered over the sunglasses and then she realized he wasn't a stranger a car away but Patrick at her own beloved T-bird. "Holy crow and Mary," said Angela. She dropped her cargo into the trunk.

He wore a white T-shirt; it was not any white T-shirt but possibly French and in perfect contradiction to his dress pants which were perhaps linen, hung loosely by a corded linen belt, preppy, clean. He smiled at her.

"Nice car," he said. "I figured you'd drive something cool like this. You're not the BMW type." He touched its waxy fender. "This is way better."

The spacious quiet of the parking lot was punctured by cars started here and there. She closed the trunk, burning her hand. Her first instinct was to hide her domesticity from him.

"Funny thing, seeing you," she said. Wings in her vision; then she heard the helicopter, thick wood drum sound of pheasant a vibration in the black asphalt. It got unspeakably loud. They looked up together when it passed over, shadowing them with its many arms, the chassis painted X66FM, black on red. It circled the parking lot. Angela's eyes hurt. She focused on him. "Must be doing a remote," said Patrick, handling the words, his casual trinkets.

He leaned on her car door. And suddenly Angela was seeing them from the air, their two heads, the circles interpreting the more complicated curves and diagonals of their bodies.

When it was quiet again, he said, "Listen Angela, I don't want to pester you. I needed to talk and I couldn't wait for an appointment." He laughed, it would be absurd, an appointment. "That's the kind of guy I am, see?"

"I'm beginning to get the picture," she said.

"When I want something, I don't wait for tomorrow."

"I'm in a hurry," she said.

"Hey, don't let me hold you up." He surrendered, cowboy-style, arms above his head. Angela moved cautiously, jumped back laughing when Patrick's hand arced through the air, a golf swing. He bowed, "Madame," and opened her door. A sidewinder, she slipped in. He closed the car door gently as someone who knows the latch. Stuck his head in the window. "Listen Angie," he began.

"Don't. Don't call me Angie. Don't do that. Look, I gotta go." Started her car. Patrick leaned in further, reached across her, his arm brushed her breast. He switched on the radio, tenor sax or was it car horns, big band, the crispness of the attack. The horns so loud, he played it too shrill, Patrick leaning into her car, she saw his smooth throat, muscled neck, he cut his hair short around the ears and nape, let it grow long on top, smell of gel, his mouth, how it changed shape. He pulled her hair, his fist full of her red hair pulling her head back, and exposed her neck, his mouth moving over her and the sound coming from his mouth on her throat a vibration almost beyond hearing. Those horns screamed and the big band tempo the virtuoso tempo. But Angela's face opened in a grimace, you could see all the teeth, you could have seen her as an old woman, the way her face was breaking in pain's smile. She pushed his face out of the window and Patrick saying, OK doll it's OK baby look baby no problem. The shift was on the steering column, she shoved it in reverse, she saw Patrick cross his arms. But it was when he shook his head like Angela was a dumb broad in traffic, she decided to kill him. He lived in play-land. Let him play dead. She was sitting on the accelerator when she jammed it into drive so the car nearly jumped on top of him and it was something like a cinematic dance step, his leap to the roof of the tin car beside him, must have scratched it bad but he was standing on the asphalt again when she saw him in the rearview, she looked back into the mirror to see if he'd gone down, even though she knew she'd missed him. He was laughing, laughing gently, like she'd just won him.

She drove home. Her face was working itself between conversations and laughter. She hadn't felt so stimulated in years. All the other games were dry compared to this quirky two-step with Patrick. A different kind of intelligence. Most unusual. A funny story. How to make it into a funny story.

She didn't know Sam would be home. He had said he was going to work all Saturday to clear up the mess Ren had left behind when he skipped out to Thailand or wherever the hell he'd flown to. She'd wait to tell Sam what had happened. It wasn't quite a story yet. She knew he was somewhere in the house. She took her time, putting the fish in the fridge. Poured a gin and tonic. Slow down girl.

The house was under the spell of a sweet moist summer afternoon. Hot days and night showers had forced summer to ripeness near decay, the dahlias she'd planted and the cut flowers, you could see the bubbles on slim stems of zinnias through the glass vases. Walking upstairs, the small sucking sound of her bare feet on varnish, she was overcome by homesickness.

She had put a screen in the corner they called her office, so that she could work while Sam was sleeping. Now she saw his head over the screen. He would be bent over her desk. Angela recalled her talent for marriage; her ability to let her irritation go, like a fist released, she would let go and the irritation would fly off, and she did this when she saw Sam at her desk. Then he disappeared. She heard the shutter on a camera, and the automatic advance. He was standing with his camera in his hands when she walked quietly around the screen (it was a white screen, like Marlene Deitrich used in *The Blue Angel*, it let in the light, milky, opaque as the petals of white gladioli). She startled him and when he flinched Angela felt the panic of a wife who despises her husband for the first time.

"What're you doing Sam?"

"Hey baby. You sneaking up on me?"

"No. I just didn't know what you were doing."

Sam shrugged and looked at the number of exposures left on the roll. "Just thought I'd take some pictures Angel." He lifted the camera. "Let's see a smile baby. Seems like years since I saw you smile."

She reached to him, put her hand over the lens.

"You'll smudge the lens, Angie."

Angela wanted to be held. Maybe Sam would be big enough to hold her. This was one of her private measurements; their relation varied quantitatively. When he did put his arms around her, and he had to do this or fall backwards, Angela running into him, at last, into his shirt, the little camera cut her back and she enjoyed this keenly, as someone who will find relief in pain. "Sam," she said, "something very strange happened today."

"I know, baby, I know." He leaned her into her chair and pushed her legs apart and began to comfort her or speak into her so his voice was a vibration. Angela watched Sam place the camera on the floor just under her desk, and even the murmurings between her legs, while she let them melt her and she played with the bristle at Sam's neck, and the thunder was it? Thunder or a train far away, a bass running under the yellow spasms collecting where Sam spoke to her, while her knees folded over the arms of the chair and her star-shaped body shone from the single point of Sam's mouth on her, Angela wanted Sam to tell her what good is it what good does it do anybody anyway? What good is it Sam? And Sam wouldn't say anything any more than it was good and she was good, wasn't she Angie, wasn't Angie good?

Agency

Angela said she didn't mind. It was painless and fine and it didn't take long. The crew had finished by the time she got home from work. They had seized the brightest hours when the sun at its zenith filled the house with light, selected the rich pigments, provoked the subtle weaves and brush strokes with absolute transparency. Sam's house had been kept like a secret, with a secret's potency, hidden by the trees and the private drive, open for the occasional party. When he kept it to himself, the place was a work of art. Angela was confused by Sam's abrupt hunger for publicity. It felt like a fire sale, the way he emptied his home of its private value.

"Some journalists are coming tomorrow. They're doing a piece on the house," he told her.

Angela looked at him, head to the side like a dog understanding human wishes. "You've never let anyone see this place."

"Sure I have," said Sam.

"Sam! Fifty people have asked to do a media number on

you. No one has ever taken a picture. You have never let anybody come close before." She was enunciating each word crisply.

"I don't know what you're talking about," he said. "You're such a wreck these days, Angie."

"I'm a wreck!" She looked around the room, seeing it as if it were already in a magazine. It had never before appeared so stylish. She went upstairs to her desk. "I'm a wreck," she said again. Her office was increasingly her refuge; she was a house pet with limited access. He had told her that he'd been taking photographs of every room to get used to the idea before the magazine people arrived. Angela stood in front of her desk and looked at the scattered words there. She tried to see her personal things with the eyes of a stranger. Maybe it was because she was in love with her work and the skill it took to construct a legal argument, but to her eyes the handwriting looked sexy, the written phrases and the simple mass of work that was evident, it was attractive, it had power. And it was a personal attribute, part of her body. Angela saw herself there and was fascinated by her own image.

Sam was a great help to the cameramen, advising them on filters as if he were director of photography. Angela met them on their way out, their arms loaded with sleek black boxes, chrome tripods, white umbrellas collapsed neatly. Only the print media remained, in the person of Cassie O'Sullivan, lifestyle columnist for the full-colour architectural magazine out of Dallas. It was the magazine's philosophy to provide a profile of the architect behind the façade, and in this case, how interesting that an amateur architect had built such an unusual house. The editors from Texas were excited about Sam.

Sam had a flickering presence, there and not there at all, charismatic and self-effacing. He presented to Cassie O'Sullivan his sinewy opinions with just the right degree of indifference. He didn't spill all over her. Cassie O'Sullivan admired his savvy, and his slim waist. Cassie had too much confidence to resent his discreet wife Angela, tastefully subdued, casual but not careless, it must be said, very elegant in a white tailored suit by Alfred

Sung, a Canadian designer, but very sophisticated. It served as a humbling reminder: style knows no borders.

When the journalist departed and they were once again alone, the summer evening dappled and sweet, Sam and Angie were surprisingly stilted with one another, as people too abruptly intimate after a public occasion, embarrassed at their recent display, their adroit exposure. "That wasn't too bad," said Angela. "She was quite nice." Sam said yes she was. It seemed an extravagance beyond even a slick journal from Texas to send such a team to Canada, but they would no doubt cover other houses, other architects, amateur and otherwise. "They were patronizing us, Sam," said Angela.

"Were they? The photographer thought he was in Minnesota." And he smiled.

They took their drinks out to the deck. Sam stoked the fireplace. "Nice, tonight," she said. His fine silhouette compelled her, his precise and compact shadow. Silence like any abstinence gathered an errant form of potency, peaceful for a few moments, and then, total. Homesick. She wanted back in. Even now, sitting beside him, she felt as if Sam were a memory of a husband, his warmth and breath and scent, knowing him there. Her chest began to hurt. The pain chiselled down her arm, into the bone, through tendons beneath the soft white skin to hostile ventricles and arteries that make a pulse hurt like water through a damaged sluice. She felt her tentative grasp of the world, and the exertion it took to fill heart with blood and lungs with air, and the easeful alternation between inhalation and exhalation became conscious, more dangerous than forgetting right from left, push from pull. She had to tell Sam about Patrick. A story like a trail of breadcrumbs.

I had been at the store with my arms full of slippery things for you when he appeared, the words in Angela's mind, they were spoken inside her skull.

"I haven't slept since Saturday," she told him. She could make her voice small, retracting. It had always been, when Angie got small, Sam got big. "This insomnia is from a kind of shock," she said.

Sam sat in the dark listening like prey, excessively still.

"I think I'm in shock somehow," she said. "It's repetition, keeps repeating."

Sam spoke slowly. "What keeps repeating, Angela?"

"Patrick showed up while I was running errands."

Sam listened.

"It kind of took me by surprise."

"Why is that?"

"I don't know."

"Is this guy nuts?"

"No. Not at all. I don't know why it got to me. Anyway. He says he needs a lawyer for some business he's starting."

"You don't do that kind of work. Or are you making some changes?"

"Work's work."

"No. It isn't."

She had an impulse to empty her pockets. When she spoke, she opened her hands for him, and her face opened, her voice high in pitch. "I wish we'd talk more," she said.

And I can't tell you that fear felt like pleasure, he was so entirely himself it made me need to break in. But now I'm here with you Sam yes it's dark but you see me here Angela very simply your wife. All of me here with you tonight, look, I'll empty my pockets on this table shine your light. Then Sam said, "We have to watch what we wish for. Don't we." She had wished for Patrick. She couldn't afford to say any more. Things were coming from behind, unintentional, why couldn't they invent their innocence and begin there? Like they used to. She yearned to do this.

He moved at ease. Dry night. No mosquitoes, very strange. The leaves made a sibilance. Sam said, "This has been very nice. But I'm going to bed, Angie. Are you staying up?" He walked freely, with grace, he put his jacket around her. "Do you want more wood?" She didn't answer him. She opted for a bitchy recalcitrance. Sam kissed her good night and went to the house. She called out to him, his hand on the door, yellow spotlight full of moths.

"We should go away for a while. Would you like to?" Sam stood with his hand on the door in the yellow light mixing moths, door, night, with his back to her, listened to her appeal, then turned slowly to face her.

"We could try," he said. Then he shrugged, tired, entered the house, the door closing, her last sight of him a tired man home to bed.

Impossible to tell distance in the dark. Too tired to get up, she lay on the chaise, watched the fire burn out. She had over-reacted again. Marriage has a way of detracting from your self-esteem, or any kind of understanding, a kind of madness living in one place with only one person to tell you what it's like out-side. Sleep by the fire tonight. Empty the space between herself and Sam. Like the impulse to clear out strange creatures when you're outnumbered, squirrels in the yard, that impulse to clear them out. Simple numbers. A warm place. Distance from Sam. Patrick's muscled neck. Very nice, she thought, she must have learned that attitude from reading James Bond novels when she was a kid. Dozed. She was responsible for Sam. Always and incessantly. The shadow of his house carved against the night. Word for it. Obsidian. Obvious. Soft applause, leaves in the breeze. Gratuitous gestures, a phone call, lunch, friendship. Make friends with him. Grow up. Big girl like me. Time is appalling. The simple duration of her marriage. Can't screw up. Too many panels on Women and the Law. Take control. She wouldn't lose. Too much agency too much education. Patrick would be her secret. Her secret. And Sam's.

The dew woke her. When she went up to bed, he was sleep-ing on his side, still as stone. She was cold so she cupped him in her legs, pulling her cool belly against the warm small of his back. The birds were beginning their alarm in the blue granite light. It would be a while before sunrise. But she slept lightly. And Sam was oblivious. She envied him for that.

Cyberspace

Sam went to find Ren in the ellipses of the Internet. Someone in Taiwan informed him Ren was in Hong Kong. Sam knew this was true and untrue: no one is in Hong Kong; it's an airport, a turnabout, everybody's there for twenty-four hours. It was a fibre optics sighting. Sam stayed on the Internet all afternoon. Ren turned up in Bombay, Bangkok, and Beijing. Sam began to feel responsible for the determinacy of his search. Just when he became aware of the concatenation of *B*s, Ren turned up in Sydney.

Sam had always relied on his height and his striking tuxedo-coloured hair, his own apparition, to give him a presence that would exceed the irony of strangers. And he had learned to work the phone, his vocal performance a blend of warmth and indifference. His business had been most successful during the period of conference calls. Sam was a muscle in a telephone line, but on e-mail, he was a typo. The information highway is a bad metaphor. No long road, no concrete, trees, yellow fields of mustard, salt lakes, no belly or thigh or palm of hand, no modest curve of prairie, no time zones, no hours and hours and hours when the long breath of a day's travel slips the self into hypnosis, no journey on the Internet. He couldn't breathe in digital space.

But that afternoon, Sam had a suppleness he had never had before. His skills on the computer were inadequate, but the perseverance with which he searched for his ex-partner was humble in its nature, a self-forgotten patience driven by something like love.

A contact in Singapore told him Ren was "taking it from both sides." In the import business this meant Ren was getting kickbacks from the manufacturers, it meant the factories had bribed him, it meant their prices weren't competitive, it explained why Sam's biggest clients had taken their patronage elsewhere, it meant Ren had been cheating Sam for the last seven years.

Ren had many "associates" with whom he had everything in common. Same age, interests, high income, same computer skills, talent for travel, same physique, and on the telephone, the same, nearly feminine, voice. On e-mail, they all sounded identical: busy, cool, angelic.

Somebody in Seoul told him Ren was dead. Must have been a good friend to hide Ren like that. In any case, Ren was beyond Sam's skills in tracking. Even through the uninflected type on his monitor, Sam could hear the amusement of Ren's colleagues, a kind of typographical laughter. His clumsy messages seemed like the noisy aggression of a rich game-hunter tracking a bird in a jungle.

When Sam's bank told him he would have to provide funds to service the company's overdraft, Sam so thoroughly saw the largesse of Ren's betrayal it altered his vision as if he were cured of forethought and hindsight. Ren had robbed him blind. Never again would Sam trust anyone to tell him even the time of day. Sam's reality became entirely of his own making. Now he needed only the strength to make it.

Making Friends

Her body was white as lily, bone in sun. But the flesh and muscle that move the somatic, the inert frame (how they would find her bones, Angela often thought about this, many years hence, perhaps reassemble the woman, attach plastic muscle, colourcode vein from artery, calculate probable weight and age at the time of death), the frame of the woman knit by cartilage and clothed, beautifully clothed in flesh, in her favourite posture, behind the wheel, like being at her desk with the text in Technicolor. But so bland the streets, bleached by more than sun.

Sam owned a piece of this development, discrete rows of tax shelters, very prestigious executive living, peace fortified by sound barriers, freeway far beyond. The houses of yellow brick like dormered sand castles and very wide black streets curved cloverleaf with long driveways over an acre of lawn, not a pock on the asphalt was there, and every road spade-shaped for neat drainage. The heat in the car forming salt licks, heat like unshed skin, heat so extreme it seemed a deprivation of the senses. This was Patrick's turf. She had learned that he lived here with his parents who must be elderly.

She told him she had called on a whim. "My turn," she said. "Wondered if I could make an appointment."

Patrick had been friendly and open. "Great," he said. "But I don't know if I should leave my mum and dad. Why don't you come here?"

"Great!" said Angie, master of oratory. Was he always ahead of her? He was like her second language. But she could be a fast study. Domesticate things. Good. A friendship. Part of her ordinary life. Good.

She said, "You scared me the other day."

Dead air; he might have been lighting a cigarette or tying his shoes. "Yeah, I know." Then that boy's laugh. "You're a jittery woman."

"Caffeine," she said.

"No," said Patrick. "That was my fault."

"It's OK."

"That was dumb to kiss you."

"Not really."

She was entertaining an ambivalence, a passivity she knew to be dangerous. Into the shimmering space she would assert herself. And swim in mid-air.

There wasn't a wrinkle in the sky, and all the Midwest's oil had been piped into the brand new streets. The houses had porticos and four-door garages. It was a neighbourhood guarded by wrought-iron gates with security posted like a lifeguard at Victoria Beach or a soldier nostalgic for the Berlin Wall. DRIVE SLOWLY WE CHERISH OUR CHILDREN. Not a convenience store in sight.

The rococo sign of a distinguished builder of fine homes remained on the lawn where the street dimpled into a bicycle-friendly curb. Must be distinguished, so illegible a sign. Signs everywhere. YOUR NEIGHBOURS ARE WATCHING. Fixed to the magnificent garage. GUARD DOG. I get the point. Parents indeed elderly. Joined at the hip, they answered the door, their geriatric entertainment. His father and mother pallid and identical. Such are the virtues of attrition, one partner upon the other, an eventual erosion of distinctive features. Both called her Dear, which she had always loved. Both called for Patrick, who bounded down the stairs, emperor of veneer. Several moments empty of intention, his parents apparently trained to take at face value their son's consistency. His mother, stooped and hesitant, led the way to the sunny space too vast to be called kitchen, establishing Angela's visit either informal or inconsequential. Like a musician playing from the wrong score, Angela's conversation too quick, too earnest, an illegitimate solo comprised of questions about their home, how long have they lived there, do they like it, yes, not long, very nice, Angela's approbation curtailed by an efficient drill, Patrick's mother's innocent and softly gnarled hand upon a Braun blender blending curds then poured thickly into green Spanish glasses and served at the white breakfast nook. A health drink, said Patrick's father winking, You'll never get an aneurysm, he toasted all.

His mother's face was peach-skin stitched to small white ears. She offered coffee cake. Patrick, for the first time, fidgeted. "Coffee cake makes me think of car coats," said Angela. She sought conspirators, Patrick and his father chewing and washing their mouths with glutinous health drink, Angela guilty over the familiar impulse to sacrifice the mother, has always paid dividends, but surely at her age she would have moved beyond. Loyalty. Mother chewing; a mouth that would predate root canal. Why is silence not golden? Angela's nerves, unweaned from caffeine, yearned for Coke, the global fix. Then Patrick's father's sneeze. Angela, pleased, looked into Patrick's shingle-blue eyes, seeking confirmation, met none. Back to you Dad. And Patrick's father, bless him, took the ball.

"Bless me," he said. And blew his Presbyterian nose in a yellow paper napkin. "Reminds me of a story Frank told this morning."

"George teed off at six a.m.," said Patrick's mother proudly.

"Frank lost his temper," said George to wife, a *voir dire.*

"That's why he loses," said expert wife, and the tautological evidence against Frank entered the transcripts of their marriage, valid, clearly.

"Anyway"—George on track—"this is a funny story. There was once a farmer in Waboden."

Patrick's mother licked her finger, gummed cake crumbs, thinking.

"And this farmer was talking to his horse. His horse was pulling the harrow you know. That's how we used to do it."

Angela woke, the chimes of real information, like a perfume ad, extrasensory: father on farm. The barefoot image fading. Patrick crossed pleated pant legs, yellow socks dipping in loafers.

"And this man's horse does something wrong. I can't quite recall what, but Frank told it pretty good. Anyway, this horse screws up."

Angela's spine curled as a comma, opening internal file, Polite Vernacular, accepted *screw up* into file.

"This is a terrible joke," said Patrick's mother, rigorous. But this too was acceptable, censure at a kitchen table.

"So the farmer says—like to the horse eh?—That's one. And the horse does something wrong again, and the farmer says, That's two, and then the horse you know does another wrong thing and the farmer says, That's three, and he shoots the horse. So he goes home for dinner. Oh and he kills a whole bunch of other animals in between. It's a long joke."

"Frank always had a good memory for long jokes," said Patrick's mother, thinking. Angela looked for irony, found none.

"Anyway, the farmer goes home to his wife and she's cooking dinner. And what does the wife do but she burns dinner. So the farmer, he says, That's one."

His yellow eyes on Angela. "Oh George," his wife gathering dishes. Tectonic plates shifted slowly, released from his eyes a ray of desperation. Angela produced laughter. She looked to Patrick who was tapping his spoon, long arms distended, the body set back in the chair, equestrian posture, and in his face, calm attention to his own distinct beating, echo, echo of his own enviable calm.

"Well Daddy, we'd better get a move on," said Patrick's mother. "We're playing doubles at three," she informed her son.

"Did you ever play hockey?" asked Angela.

"Who? Paddy? Not my boy. Thank heavens no. There's not a scar on him. But he's an expert tennis player, isn't he Daddy." Arms full of dishes, his mother squeezing between Patrick's chair and the glass cupboards left a space the span of a fist between belly in sweatsuit and son, Patrick, perfect man. They would have to hurry, only a short drive, we usually walk. It was nice to have met her, yes. Much younger, Patrick's parents in pastel leisure suits and tennis shoes, opening the aluminum door which led through breezeway to twin Accords, walked on their toes in the heat.

Patrick let the water run into the sink. He stood gazing and played his fingers pizzicato back and forth until it was running clear and cold. He offered a drink to Angela. They stood at the sink and drank the cold water. This was a conspiracy at last and precious as sleep. The adults had departed and the true and spectral day would begin.

"I remember a friend I had when I was young, a little girl about thirteen or so who would have parties in a house that was about this size but old like the houses in the part of town where the grain merchants lived. She was very pretty and smart and rather bad. There's a kind of genius in that. She's had four husbands now. I like her. Anyway she would invite us to her house for these mixed parties, we called them, mixed meant I wore, that is, I wore whatever, my mother—" The story slipped out her hands for a moment while Angela recalled the bra her mother had given her to wear to the mixed party with boys. She picked it up. "Her house had a third storey which was her ballroom, and in the cloudy afternoon, we danced to 'Norwegian Wood.' What I saw of the world for my first seventeen years was what I could glimpse over a boy's shoulder. Or when you're tucked under his arm, everything gets tilted over on an angle."

Patrick listened and drank his water. He gestured with his elbow to the door. "They shouldn't play in this heat."

Angela was at speed. "Oh they play outside? I didn't know."

Patrick nodded. "Clay courts."

"Clay is nice."

Patrick nodded. "Slows the game."

He ran the water and refilled his glass and drank.

"That's why they like it," he said. "They can see the ball."

"Well that would help I guess."

Patrick slapped at a mosquito and opened his hands. He placed the splayed cartoon body on the kitchen counter.

On Patrick's face, a point of blood small as a spore or a taste bud, the blood shining nearly black. They were standing at the kitchen counter on a summer day in the middle of the afternoon. She wore a sundress. It would soon be time to leave.

Her shoulders had freckles connected. Same colour as her hair, red freckles like the inside had surfaced. But if you could erase them, the skin would be white as paper. If you could. How old she must be, but nothing like other women whose skin showed indentations the way the ground looks from an airplane, how small a river or a minute on someone's skin. "How old are you?" he asked. "Thirty-seven," she said, with the boldness fresh to women since age had no longer been a factor. I'm thirty-seven. That's final.

"You never had any kids."

"Well not yet anyway."

He teased her. "Isn't that kind of old for having kids?"

Clock chiming. Angela laughed and then you could make out the places where the lines will be.

"I'm an old lady," she said. "Anyway. I just came to clear things up a little."

"And you did," said Patrick, smiling.

"Your parents are nice."

He nodded. It seemed the end of the interview.

"Well I really am sorry for the way I acted the other day." She walked toward the front door. Patrick walked behind her. When one is singular, air closes after you like wake. She had too much skin. He held the door. The heat entered the house like soldiers. Angela turned toward the street. Her eyes were dilated. The sharp light entered her skull. On the street, the sound of a car driven fast. She tied herself to a perception: standard shift, old British make. The familiar motor-sound placed her at home hearing Sam arrive. Her pupils were too open; the heat was a white tongue. She returned several steps toward Patrick's open door, involuntarily seeking shelter. Everyone has a part of them that's uncarved and lumpish, a portion undisciplined by the dance. Her back when she turned to Patrick's cool entry was thickly fleshed, the pink untannable flesh of a redhead. She pivoted on one foot. The pale toes gripped her sandals, one toe curled up like a short finger. The car geared down, then sped away. Against the cool recess of his parents' home, Patrick was clear as a photograph. All his attention was focused on the street. Then he looked at her. His face was compassionate. "Your husband just drove by," he said.

Dreaming

more intimate, a scrutiny he'd call love

Then she was awake. Her eyes were open in the dark. She looked alert when she sat up and she didn't know Sam's eyes were open too when she unravelled herself from the bed. Angela walked in the dark. When she returned he asked her what she was doing, his voice close and smooth.

"Nothing," she said. "I had a dream."

"What was your dream?"

"Oh," said Angela, perhaps reluctant. "I was on a ship you know and they were putting a coffin into the sea. The water was dark blue but kind of light from inside. They dropped this coffin into the sea and then someone said, Now you can live in the imagination. Then I woke up because I had to go to the bathroom."

"That was a sad dream. Why were you having a sad dream?"

Angela was falling asleep. "No"—she was sleep-drunk—"it was a good dream. It was really good."

"You should write it then, in your little book."

PART TWO

Blue

At ten o'clock on a June night, the indigo sky absorbed what was left of the light in the room. Through the glass you could see a single elm, thick and broad, blown and bent as the palm of wind blew away the surface of things. It stood elevated against the storm clouds, below it the long fence grown over by creeper vines. In this light which was dyed by the charge in the air, the red berries seemed big and promising.

When you turned your back to the window, you were quite blind. Silence was a moat around the house, a barricade beyond which noise pressed. A pause created by your own hand. You sat on her bed, moved her leg out of the way, her foot against the bedclothes snagged and the leg was bruised and the peace from your hand was cupped around the house. She lay within, her breath secretive and apocryphal and shallow.

Privacy is a treasure few of us want, a lost currency. Real solitude would be swollen with all the voices, true solitude would have a tooth for every word spoken, a feather for every feeling of love or jealousy or hatred, and in its indifference it would reach a claw and gracefully extinguish her breathing.

She couldn't define the disturbance. The presence of a stranger walking the passages of the house. A bird or a snake would be more explicit, more traceable. He travelled from room to room, in his hands and in his pockets keepsakes and mementos, evidence of values that would exceed him. Things of this nature attached themselves to his hands. Count them and every time the sum will differ. He had cured himself of visibility. And the rage that lit his way tolerates all, consumes and grows.

He was most sensitive to duration, had a keen sense of timing, an exquisite understanding of the spatial, the gestural, nature of time. The house was wide and he had swept it. Later he would find a mirror and amuse himself with his own elliptical eyes. Rain pressed the small faces of leaves against the glass. She was awake. She was feeling her bruises, sitting in bed like a sick child. She looked up and he was standing at her door. Her life was a talisman he would put under his tongue.

Peace

he asked me, whose name will you utter when
you are most lost?

There was mud on her left knee from when she'd stumbled hurrying across her garden. He reached forward to brush it away and then stopped himself as if he'd nearly interfered with evidence. She had come to tell him of her adventure with Patrick. Sam was fixing his boat at the dock. It was still very hot that evening. You could smell the barbecues from the families who fished on the blond banks across the water, behind them the rye grass waving.

Sam's property looked vulnerable from the river. Angela was always surprised by the sudden exposure to the wide and sullen water. When she walked down the steep stairway, her hand tightened on the railing, determined, faltering, a stubborn hesitancy familiar to Sam. The soft grey wood dock made a low hollow sound underfoot. They spoke about repairs in the cockpit of Sam's sailboat, looking out across the river to the small figures fishing and watching them from the opposite shore. Then he said he'd like a swim. Sam helped Angela as she stepped out of the boat. She tried to retain his hand when they went up, but the stairs were too narrow.

He splashed cold water on his neck. It ran down his back and dampened the waist on his shorts as he sat by the pool, shaded and receptive to Angela's story. Sam had acquired a miniature jade dog carved in Indonesia which appeared to be significant as a charm; he kept it with him as one would keep worry beads and when his wife began to speak he brought forth the little dog and examined it with his fingers.

Disparate birds driven by a singular hunger gathered on the hawthorn. "He's really quite nice," Angela was saying, her eyes on the birds. "He lives in that new development west of town. His house is barely finished. I can't tell where they would have lived before that. Everything I could see was new. I mean, not just new, but you know that stuff you can buy without any kind of style but nouveau-new? The tables don't have any edges, everything's kind of curved and it doesn't even try to imitate another period, Louis Quinze dining-room suites, none of that, just, new. It's a good thing there was air conditioning or the stuff might've melted, like it was made out of wax."

Sam held the jade dog in his palms and reclined, so calm you couldn't see him breathe.

"It's like they've all been boiled, stringy, the skinniest family I've ever seen. Even the old mother, her arms, christ her fingers were muscled. That looks so weird in an old woman. I'm glad I'm fat. At least I won't get that gristle on my throat. I almost wanted to touch it, that's obscene I know, but it was the weirdest skin. She's in great shape. They went off, his dad and mum, they went to play tennis. But first we had this wretched avocado drink, I don't know if it was really avocado but. He's a nice young guy, not very smart, apparently a nearly pro tennis player, I might play with him, we might play sometime, or you should Sam, you'd give him a game. He apologized for the way he acted the other day so I think everything's going to be fine. I don't know why I got freaked out. I'm drinking too much coffee. And Marlene's murder threw me. Well I guess it would. Obviously. Anyway. I'm glad I went. He's just a young guy. It's good I went. It wasn't really fun, but it was nice to talk to somebody who isn't a lawyer. I mean next to you."

She sighed or her breath caught in her heart, post-confessional contentment. Sam placed the jade dog on the glass table in the shifting light from the swimming pool. He did this decisively as if it were a painful but necessary renunciation. Then he stood and slipped out of his shorts. There was flesh around his hips. The thighs and calves had thick knots of muscle, and though he was too tall to be fat, the flesh was unfocused. He stood at the edge of the diving board, balanced by his hands which he held perpendicular to the pool, the veins of water moving on him. He was so sure and naked, she looked away. She asked him, "You drove by?" And then the neat white fluorescence where he had dived.

It was a night of silence and opposites. Summer solstice. Sam and Angela had dinner late. She cooked well that night. She cut red pepper and sugar peas and sea bass with strawberry vinegar, the hypnosis of a knife cutting chilled food in her hands. Sam had taken up a new hobby, polishing stones on a drafting table which he'd set in the centre of the kitchen close to where she cooked. The sun set while they ate. Then they roamed their separate paths through the house, their indifference like timelessness or innocence and their faces were their sleeping faces. The house fell into darkness disturbed only by the precision of his spot lamp. Dusk stretched to a fine powder, a dusting of light which would never entirely fail, it would yawn into an eggshell dawn while they worked at their individual leisure, never looking into one another's faces but reading the curved shoulder, a word spoken but not for anyone's hearing.

Angela had been lying on the floor with her back and neck supported by the red pillows. In one hand she held open a book, the other hand combing through her hair. Her eyes travelled over many pages. The important thing was a casual posture. Her stomach cramped, a low-gauge dread. Sometimes Angela's unease was a reaction to their freedom from necessity, to choose to read or polish stones or take a bath. She would take a bath.

When she opened the cedar cupboard to fetch a bar of soap she discovered the henna she'd stored there last winter. She would put the henna in her hair tonight, though it would have to sit an hour. She would open wine and listen to music while it worked in its vegetative way upon her hair, an indulgence for the shortest night of the year, to look after herself in private. She closed the door. The bathroom was small with a slanted cedar ceiling and a recessed window.

When Sam found her, the henna was washing from her hair and down her body, flood waters in the delta, the henna running over her breasts as she stood in the shower with her arms raised to her head washing the root-smelling dye from her hair so her breasts lifted and he thought they resembled the milk-tits of a young woman or the nudes they had seen at the Louvre, breasts with the visible flesh beneath the nipple, breasts without the place beneath to hide his fingers, the water running over her red as if she were washing all the colour from her hair.

Lewis

Angela sat beside Joey in the visiting room of the Remand Centre and watched television. It was nine o'clock. The couch was covered in brown chenille and the room was painted orange. Joey enjoyed his television hours (he was allowed only two hours each evening) and seemed particularly engaged by the commercials. She was falling between the lank cushions with the pennies and broken crayons, leaning against Joey, mesmerized by the liturgical sound track, the morbid TV light. She began to watch by accident and her fascination had the prohibited quality of overeating.

The couch comprised the only furniture and the television was the only window in a rectangular room designed to inspire passivity, to sedate its inhabitants and prevent not only escape but any mental process other than the automatic, like a life-support system, a dialysis machine. Angela fell into watching as she would fall into sleep while being driven on a long journey on an overcast day.

Two men were talking in front of an elevator shaft. One man

wore a suit and the other wore overalls with oversized pockets
containing keys and screwdrivers. When the repairman brought
the cage down to eye-level, there was the nude body of a sexy
and large-boned young woman with short blonde hair and electrical tape over her mouth. It was silver electrical tape, like
lycra. She had been cut, thinly, the black blood fresh, ear to ear,
her blue eyes open wide.

She was one of a series. The chief detective, a serious, powerful man striped by venetian blinds, stood behind his desk. He
asked his lieutenant if she had been raped. "There are no signs
of penetration," said the righteous black cop. Angela watched,
Joey watched. Their watching conveyed a familial resemblance
to their faces. The murderer lived with his wife in an apartment.
Over the frail shoulder of his plain, Midwestern, religious, and
faithful wife, Angela and Joey examined the Polaroids, four
small detailed photographs of women's backs, hands tied
behind with electrical cord, their yellow flesh. One woman
stared at the camera, the articulate inscription around her neck.

Angela's tongue rested on the bottom of her mouth.
Together, they looked at the credits, mouths open, sequential
ads. She woke up at the start of the next show, in her mouth the
percussive taste of wood. When she sat up, stretched, she met
the disinfected world. Joey's face from the side, round cheeks,
baby fat like chicken fat under his chin. She placed her palm
beneath his face. He knocked her hand away so hard his nails
cut her cheek just beneath her eye. Angela moaned from deep
inside, a lumbar utterance shuddered at its edges.

Joey looked like he wished to take it back because he didn't
know what it was he'd given. He was afraid of her. His fear was
contagious. She stood and walked about dramatically, glamorous and well dressed and, of course, accustomed to injury.
The cut looked like lipstick. He watched her as if his eyes were
on a leash.

"That was an accident, Joey. We'll just forget it."

He said nothing, watching.

"I want you to know, it hurt." It was her duty, the victim
should respond, make known a correct version of her pain.

Physical. Result of an accident. Apologize to your lawyer. She switched channels, cop show to family sitcom. She placed herself between him and the TV, arms akimbo, kitchen posture. Ingenious interrogator, Angela took a fresh approach, empathetic and blunt. "Joey, are you all right?" Inviting him to make a fresh start, no congenital defects in their relationship.

He shrugged, revealing the faint infra-red of rebellion. She drew up a chair.

"Let's take it from the beginning."

He looked past her to the television. She turned it off; time to do your homework young man.

"That's my favourite show."

Angela took several moments to laugh while Joey waited patiently.

Joey was a patient boy.

"Joey do I really need to tell you how serious this is? Now tell me what happened."

"I told it already."

"But tell me. I'm your friend."

"You're a lady lawyer."

"Yes. I am. And I'm going to help you."

"You know the Ex? Like the Red River Ex."

"Oh yes. Yes, I do," said Angela, pleased. A telephone was ringing in another room and her spirits rose automatically.

"You know those things that grab toys? Like for a quarter? You put in a bunch of quarters and it kind of grabs this claw thing at the toys. Like they're just little stuff."

Joey demonstrated with his hand, a claw-thing. Angela remembered the fair and the game he was describing. She saw herself standing before the miniature loader trying to manipulate the bucket to clasp a plastic toy.

"Oh yeah!" she said. It was nice to be speaking off-topic.

"Well that's where I was when I went to that lady's house."

"Before?"

"Yeah."

"You were at the Red River Ex?"

"Yeah."

"For how long?"

"I don't know. Couple of days."

"But on that day. On the day you went to the lady's house, how long were you at the fair?"

He didn't know, he was at the Ex for a few days. When did he go to the lady's house? He wasn't sure, it was getting dark because the lights were nice on the Ferris wheel. The lights on the ride were on when he went to her house. Why did he go to her house? Because Lewis asked him to. Who is Lewis? Some guy. He doesn't know. Had Lewis been drinking? Yeah. Had Joey been drinking? Yeah. Is he a big boy? Who, me? No, I mean is Lewis a big boy. Yeah. Is Lewis a man? He doesn't know. That would be up to Angela, Lewis's masculinity. But that's not the point.

"Tell me what happened. You went to her house after the fair."

"I was sleeping at the Ex."

"On that day?"

"Well after that I never went back. Like I came here where they brought me."

She started again. How did he go to her house, who is Lewis, how long was he in the house, what did he do, what did Lewis do, how did the lady get so hurt, how did she get to be so hurt? Joey stood up.

"I've got to pee."

He was much taller than she had thought. He had always been sitting, and this was the first time she had seen him stand. When he was returned to her, he was very tired. He held his head in his hands.

"I'm sorry," she said. "We have to do this now."

And he told her, he had been in the lady's house. When she came downstairs he cut her with the knife.

Angela's heart was hurting. "Who is he? Who do you mean he?" And then she said, "Is he Lewis?"

Joey said, "Yeah, Lewis, he went upstairs. He and Lewis go all over her house, and then he gets mad."

"Which do you mean, Joey? You're saying 'he.'"

"Like he is, like me and Lewis. I wish we didn't go. At first I said I wouldn't do it."

"Do what?"

"He wants me to do a B and E. He says he did it lots of times before. And then first I say no. We're drinking together the night before."

"Where were your parents?"

He looked at her, seeing the distance between them. "They were out drinking those days." And then, something firming in him, "Lewis said he did it before. Killed a lady. I didn't believe him till I saw."

"Tell me what you saw."

"He takes out, like he gets mad at the lady because it's just a bunch of crap anyways."

"What happens when he gets mad? Wait a minute. Where is Lewis?"

"Like me and Lewis. I don't know his last name."

"You were both upstairs. Where was the lady?"

"Ask me what he was wearing."

"Who?"

"A black jacket and a shirt with stripes on it."

"Where was the lady in the house?"

"Upstairs. But then he goes upstairs too."

He was staring at the blank TV. She gently shook his shoulder, her voice very soft.

"He went upstairs," she prompted him.

"The cops came. Ask me about the blood now."

"Why?"

"It's part of the thing I told. Now you should do the part about the knife."

"You told the police you had a knife from your house. Did you go to your home before you went with Lewis?"

"Somebody called them. The lady called them."

"She was lying on the floor with the telephone in her hand."

"You already know?"

"I read your confession."

"I told the cops about him."

"Joey you have to concentrate."

"Lewis went out the screen where it was broken."

"Where was it broken? They're saying it wasn't broken anywhere for him to get away. Are you sure he went out through a screen?"

"Ask me what time and I say I don't know for sure."

Bovary

yours Sam, I told him. I say your name in the dark.

Angela knew much about the physics of passivity, its laws submerged in the beating of her heart, the wasted energy discharged in the form of heat during those high-cholesterol moments when she strayed from her own best interest. Her temperature rose when she told Randy that she was going to do some work at home where she could better concentrate. The deception was a stimulant. She played generic rock music loudly without hearing it and drove fast and when she got home she ate a sandwich standing in front of the fridge and went searching for contraband, Sam's cigarettes which he liked to conceal in winter suits in the cedar closet. The smoke made her ill so she took a couple of aspirins with an ounce or two of whisky. Then she shaved her legs very carefully, completely.

She phoned Regina. "Hey babe," Regina said. "I just had this Nazi in here accused of embezzlement."

"Yeah?" Angie's voice was anemic.

"The biggest reactionary dick I have ever seen. He was so arrogant I felt like his concubine. But you know? It was his shoes that really did me in. This really slippery leather. I don't know. I couldn't stop staring at his feet."

"Yeah?" Angela said again. "Weird."

"I'm confused, Mum. You want a drink or something, later? You at your office?"

"Yeah. Or not really. I just came home."

"That's nice," said Regina. And Angela could hear her flipping through paper. "So?"

"Just saying hello."

"In the middle of the afternoon. You're turning into a real housewife, you know that? I've got to make a living dollface. Ciao." Then she came back. "Hey Angie. How's the little boy?"

Angela touched her little injury, small as a paper cut. "He's kind of funny."

"Funny ha ha? Or funny in the head."

"He's maybe got a few problems. But he couldn't have done it."

Regina said, "Hold on a minute," and put her on hold. Came back, the reception cutting in mid-word, "'nother call."

"He didn't do it, for sure, no way."

"OK Einstein. Look, I've got a call. Phone me tonight." And in a singsong, "Have a nice day."

Angela stood a long time holding strands of her hair up against the sun. Then she went to her desk. She dialled Patrick. Her breathy voice. "You want a coffee?"

He hesitated. "Sure."

They agreed to meet at a place downtown. Another long drive for Angela. Very public. She likes a noisy restaurant, the action, the comfort of many people around you.

She couldn't find anything to wear. So hot today, she washed at the sink and then when she'd washed she took a shower and had half the time she needed to get downtown. It was impossible to dress for the heat without revealing too much of herself. And so she was dying in the conservative red dress she wore.

She and Patrick took a table in the centre of the restaurant, Angela aware of how her legs were crossed and the tenor of her voice and how revealing it is to open her mouth and put food in it. She drank tea and grew hotter.

Patrick didn't talk much. He ate and watched the other people at their tables with benign apathy. He seemed to be eating lightly spiced food in a sunny restaurant with a friend. Angela was examining his face intensely, she looked away when he looked up. "What?" he asked. "Nothing. I didn't say anything." What he indicated might have been mild astonishment at their acquaintance. "You're looking at me like I'm a magazine or something," he told her.

Angela laughed heartily, throwing her head back, revealed the hull-shape of her white jaw while Patrick looked on. She needed him to have an offbeat mind. She was suddenly anxious. "Are you OK?" Patrick asked her. Upon a quick and searching inquiry she discovered that she was fine, in fact, she felt happy. Like a blister, her happiness, bright. She touched his sleeve.

Outside the restaurant she hesitated, avid and delighted. He took her arm to guide her to her car. They walked out of sight down a back lane littered with styrofoam cups and blossoming weeds.

She had parked in the shade of a tree gauzy with the webs of caterpillars, she heard the worms chewing and looked up, seeking some diversionary urban wit. He pulled her to himself and began to kiss her throat. His hand moved to her breasts, a tanned hand on a red dress. She is so female and the dress is cut so finely with a seam that runs along the breasts and his dark hand, his pale as milk fingernails cut square and he is caressing her breasts, he teases at her nipples, her leg rises and cups him, his hand on her, somewhere a woman in a red dress wraps her leg around a man, she rubs the soft skin on the inside of her thigh, she rubs her skin against the fine fabric, her pink hand on the back of his shirt, these are things that will stay with you. They will, if you let them, stay.

And when images stay, it is more accurate to say, they repeat themselves. They recur. They metastasize. Don't they Sam?

Met Patrick for tea. Stop thinking about it . . .

Othello

Sam left while she was still dreaming. He went to his office very early in the morning and he stayed there till very late at night. Angela slept most deeply just before dawn. She looked like someone sleeping at the centre of a cat's eye, kept there, suspended. Beyond the singing woods surrounding the driveway, the streets were empty and wide. The moment before the sun's oblique light seemed to last forever.

The week before, Sam had fired every employee of Import Trade. He had told them he would settle with them fairly but there was no reason for them to return to work. There *was* no work. Any day now, the bank would probably call in his operating loan. He had to be invisible. If he sneezed, the deck of cards would tumble on his head. Everybody in the office was sad and angry, and some of them were threatening legal action. His severance packages were enough to put him under for good.

He hadn't mentioned any of this to Angela. He had gone home and found her peeling carrots at the sink. She'd turned to him and asked him what was wrong. She could barely manage a full stop. "Nothing," he said. "How was your day?" And Angie had given him an explicit itinerary. He had chosen then not to tell her and the secret was quickly gaining potency.

She needed him to be fine. He must be successful and happy, so that their lives could be free from weight. She loved him for being an invisible husband, a silent partner. He needed to dominate her; she knew that. He was permitted his delusion as long as he was prosperous. She fit herself beneath him and touched him with the tips of her breasts and her mouth slightly dry clung to him like she would drink from him. That was their shape. If he were to prove weak, if she were to discover him, it would destroy the balance of their erotic life. She wasn't as responsive as she seemed. He had seen her manly side, her dismissive and rational working self. He knew that she played Leda because it was a stimulant; their attraction to each other was dependent on it. She was careful in bed, to let him lead. He knew that.

She called him twice that day, once in the morning and once in the afternoon, unnaturally cheerful and brisk. When he told her he was fine, she accepted it too quickly. She was vague about her own activity. Oh, not much, she said. I might quit early. Not much doing here. What are you up to? Not much? Me neither. A nothing kind of day. She called once more before she left her own office and asked him what he would like for dinner. She sounded impatient, like someone who didn't want to go to a store and buy groceries and cook them. She sounded bored. When he said that he had to work till late, he wasn't sure she'd heard him, though he could feel a slight pulse of vivacity on the line. She was yawning when she hung up. She laughed and apologized, "Excuse me! Oh! That's awful. Well OK then, see you later."

All day, Sam had sat in a silent office. With the exception of her disinterested calls, the phone didn't ring. He knew he was maudlin, and the shame of that made it worse. He had been drinking whisky since four. He had to move. He was paralyzed by solitude. But it was too late. The sorrow made something in him crouch, seaweed on the floor of the dark ocean. When he stood, it was with the faith of an acrobat, a thin man wearing ten hats on a highwire. Don't look down. Don't look down. He wouldn't look down. But he wanted to go under. He was drinking like he'd get there.

It was uncanny. The way her eyes had the same restless distraction as Ren's. The way they both counted on you to love them. The vanity of that. Their confidence and their disregard. When Ren came to town, Angela would behave like a coquette, impatient with Sam as if he were weather, something to be accepted or overcome. When he told her that Ren had vanished, it seemed to affirm something in her, a sympathy or foreknowledge. Angela knew where Ren was. These people live somewhere in the ethereal new world, quick to grasp the day's vernacular, relieved to abandon the past, like creatures of another element whose homeopathic medicine is repetition. When Ren was there, Angela smiled and laughed with uncommon pleasure. And now that Ren wasn't with them anymore, she didn't seem to care. She moved on, like a little dog on thin ice. She acquired other friends. Patrick. Another angel. Strange and easily mollified.

Sam could hardly move. The depression was a transfusion, milk for blood. He realized he was hungry because the whisky felt cold. When he stood, he had never been so tall. How could she not be aware of what an accomplishment it was to stand when he was really a clenched fist?

It was a walk across a stone moon to reach the filing cabinet. The room was so distinct from him it curled away and stopped still when he looked. His loneliness lit him and shone painfully in his stomach. He took from the cabinet a file of xeroxed copies of Angela's handwriting. The pages had a dark crease in the middle like the soft pencil line on the centre of her belly. Her scrawl was strangely translated by the machine which had neglected the bleed of ink into the loose bond she favoured, the freedom of the cursive notation. Messages she'd sent round trip. Begging for interception. Her journal was a confession from the planet she lived on with herself. She was too delicate, too needy, to make them to him directly. Theirs was a circuitous communication.

Sam read Angela's journal like someone memorizing his own tattoo. When he was away from it, he could never remember her precise words and this amnesia made him an addict for the private performance, to stand here in the middle of his office and read. As it would be for someone who can never remember his mother's kiss, kissing. With her teeth, with the marble she wore for skin. How she kissed him with that.

Sam stood before his filing cabinet and held his arms straight above him and the words tipped off the pages like glass eyes, like pennies falling into a bottomless wishing well. Pennies falling and falling through mirrors that never caught the images she'd painted there to throw back upon himself. He couldn't see his loved self anywhere. He saw his eclipse. How her words sacrificed him.

He saw she had a life entirely distinct from the submissive one she showed him. She smiled more fully, breathed more deeply, moved more freely, than the Angela that was his wife smiled, breathed, moved. He was fixed to her journal. The meaning of her entries there had the force of parable, an endless fraction. He would see, like the sun on a tin can in the woods, a glint of meaning, a quick access while he was reading, but when he put the file away she would slip off, lost in a swarm of interpretation.

But he didn't see that her desire was written into his absence, how she had placed him as an icon is placed, behind a curtain upon which is projected the endless sideshow. He didn't see the power of his own presence through omission. He was there, in his own apostrophe.

touching strangers

Angela's eyes were closed and the sun made yellow splashes behind her eyelids. She listened to the sound of birds, a swing set and children's voices, sounds of the same high pitch. Beneath her fingers where they lay on the green bench that was so hot it would melt her fingerprints, behind her blind eyes and her burning fingers, ran a race of typeface because she had spent the morning reading, the handsome serif print floating against the children's shrill noise.

She had another interview with Joey. She'd talked to his case worker, or one of them, for there seemed to be hundreds of case workers. Joey had more biographers than any politician or film star. This woman had a voice like a phone book, matter-of-fact, rational to the extreme and safely uninspired by an ideal. It made her trustworthy because she wasn't angered by Joey's deviance from a norm. She felt no outrage. Joey's world was a pervasive orphanage. It was a dark freedom. The absence of an ideal saved him from desire, but it put no shine on the world at hand.

Angela could see red with her eyes closed. It looked like yellow. The sweet grinding of the swing set etched itself around the print. Angela would not open her eyes until she'd solved the problem. It was one of her methods, this effortless meditation. How the birdsong fell a quarter of an inch like twelve-point print, how it was all the same. On a good day there was no contradiction; on a good day, there was only the work. No loose ends.

Beyond the wire fence the boys from the Centre played basketball. Joey was dodging and running. She heard his breathing. At her feet two small fat children sat face to face with their arms around each other. Sand stuck to the creases in their flesh. They were perhaps two years old, kissing, ardent, kissing with love. They were dressed in baby blue, covered with sand, and their round arms embraced the occasion of their kiss. Boy or girl, impossible to tell.

The social worker had described Joey as a product of "neglect abuse." It gave Angela the option of making him a victim of the system if they were forced to appeal but it would never come to that. All the same, the phrases for an arch defence came to mind; she would make a play on the word *foster*. Foster means to tend with affectionate care. Joey had been fostered by youth court.

He was playing with the other kids. He knew Angela as another kind of social worker, the redheaded one; her distinction was that faint coloration, brush stroke beneath the type, his "case." The other boys in the detention centre were nice when no one was watching. It was not cool to be nice. They trusted each other to be cool.

The kissing children disappeared, called by an elderly Chinese woman wearing slippers full of sand. Kind face, curved back, rose in her hair, paper rose, life is an art. Angela was drowsy and calm. Joey ran to the fence to retrieve the ball and smiled at her. She smiled complacently and he went off to play.

"Thought you were going to talk to him." The social worker was stocky, thick-limbed, very short, with thick blunt black hair. While they talked, Angela watched the woman's glasses slide down her nose made slippery in the heat and she wanted to push them back up with her middle finger. "I will," said Angela, sleepy. "I hate to stop the game."

The woman laughed, or a brief exhale, a bit surprised, finding a toy in a safe-deposit box. She kicked off a pair of thongs and played her toes in the fine black dust, leaned back to sun her ample belly and breasts. She wore a white sweatshirt with an illustration from a comic book, a glamorous brunette smacking her own forehead and the caption, "I forgot to have children!" She and Angela watched the delinquents play.

"He's doing good," the woman said, nodding.

Angela looked at her. "He's such a nice kid," she said, begging an explanation. The woman remained composed and neutral. Angela's question was endlessly deferred as if there were a delay on the debt owed to someone like this boy. Joey. A good kid. Strangely irrelevant.

Angela wanted to know whether the woman would consider Joey capable of violence. More than that she badly wanted from her a judgement; like someone walking in the dark, her hands yearned for a wall. The woman would provide not so much a judgement as a disinterested measurement, like an isobar. Angela envied her ordinary contact with ordinary things. The woman nodded again and laughed a bit at the boys' game. "Kind of amazing isn't it?" she said. "They play so good." The game was intricate, skilful, and the players obedient to the rules, in love with the imaginary limits of centre line, side line, free throw line.

The day extended itself like a child lying in the grass. There was nothing to be done. That unlimited yield of childhood. Frayed at its edges, an old T-shirt of a day, the time before knowing how to tell time, when an afternoon was delicious with boredom and whim, and intention was something that might last a city block, gazing at the sidewalk, the ants appearing, disappearing, appearing, the cracks that break your mother's back. All that was in the wide world, a boy's grimy hands on a ball, the sounds of breathing, scuffing of running shoes on the sun-whitened pavement.

"He's better here." The woman was pressed against the bench the way a pregnant woman will sit to ease the pressure on her lower spine. "I knew a kid once," she said, looking at Angela for the first time and seeing in Angela's stylish composure merely another creature, part accident part contrivance, "who begged to see his own files. He'd been a ward of the state pretty well his whole life, parents booze-freaks, mean thing at home, the video thing, pornos for breakfast and that, real mean. This kid was smart but useless, a real talent for the streets. Paranoid. Real bad paranoia. You roll over in your sleep, he thinks you're hating him in your dreams. Real bad. Blink, he thinks he's in your eye. So anyways, he wants to see his file on himself. One weekend he sneaks into my office, like this kid's such a great thief we called him Houdini. Nothing could keep him out of a place he wanted to go. I'm away for the weekend for a change." She shook her head. "Bad timing. He reads the file. It does something to his head. He goes back to his room and hangs himself. Ties his socks together and jumps off a chair."

Joey started to wrestle with another boy.

"Cut that out!" the woman yelled at them. They obeyed her. The game was briefly shadowed.

"Joey's not paranoid," said Angela.

The woman looked at her, canny and superior. These damned liberals. She looked at Angela's shoes. Liberal shoes, liberal stockings, liberal skirt, liberal voyeur, liberal fucking bleeding-heart voyeur.

"And he's not a violent kid," Angela said.

"Everybody's got it in them. Some kids, it's the only way they're going to touch somebody. If they hit them. It's like kind of information for them, you know. Contact. Cuts into the loneliness."

"Did you ever meet a boy named Lewis?"

The woman thought a minute, closing one eye. "Chubby guy? Métis? Glue?"

"I don't think so. . . ," said Angela.

"Lewis." (thinking) "Lewis." She shook her head. "Maybe."

She thought again. Snapped her fingers and pointed at Angela. "Mother did crack! Arsonist! B and E with assault! Two years secure treatment!"

Angela shook her head, doubting.

"That one got away," said the woman.

There were white moths in the grass. When the woman stood and walked to the chain-link fence and put her hands up to twine her fingers in the chain, she leaned on one hip so her thick legs formed a triangle with a motion so burlesque Angela felt dangerously close to laughing, while the woman's feet brushed through the grass and the white moths rose small and white and waved their wings as if the grass were clouds and the dusty air were sky. There was such camaraderie between the playing boys then. In their grunting taciturn game, something vastly amusing. You couldn't tell who was teamed with whom, who would win, no score, no object, the play like the patterns of wings.

"Joey threw a tantrum Tuesday night," said the woman, her short thick back to Angela. "He really lost it." She pulled her shirt away from her shoulder and revealed a bright black mark the size of a plum, punctured, teeth marks. "Thought you should know."

Angela was mad as a mother brought to task by the school, anger at the child no match for her anger at the teacher. Joey put his hand out to stop another boy from taking the ball. He pushed through and sank a basket. "Good one, Joey," the woman yelled. Joey looked toward the sound of her voice. Briefly. An irritant. He drove through the boys for the ball. She turned her face toward Angela. "You better talk. It's nearly supper." She gave a loud whistle with two fingers. "Joey! You got your interview now!" He stopped instantly, a toy turned off, and walked toward the supervisor, who took his elbow and guided him inside.

Falling Ill

Sam was ill. For two days his feet extended beneath the blankets, the bedroom loft smelling of yeast. On Wednesday, Angela went to see if he was breathing (she had been sleeping on the leather couch, which was sticky, like sleeping with a skinned animal) though she had a good idea that he was indeed alive. He had been asleep since Sunday. Angela was compelled by the depth of his dreaming.

He lay on his stomach. Angela placed her hand on his back between the shoulder blades. Sam's body was rigid. He turned his head toward her. He hadn't eaten since Sunday breakfast. Or perhaps he hadn't eaten for many days prior, Angela couldn't know. His face was bone, exaggerated by his blanched skin and black hair, by the peppered beard, the long nose, the jaw, his teeth smoke-stained. "You look like shit," she said; it was the most affectionate thing she could say. Sam had closed his eyes again and pressed his face into the mattress. "Can I get you anything?" Her refrain was like the electrical habits of a house, the white noise, her gesture an automatic reflex like digestion or blinking.

He was in the kitchen. In a bathrobe. Unshowered. Barefoot. The bald ankles and the white bulb of his heel.

Then he was cured, healthy with the fierce health of the newly risen. Never a man to carry much fat under his smooth skin, Sam's body had retained its compression and lost its flesh; he was all muscle and bone. His hand shook when he poured the eggnog. Angela wondered if she was coming down with the same flu, poisoned by the sight of the nutmeg floating.

They would go out for dinner. They would eat wonderfully. He dressed in black pants and a white shirt. With his black hair and white face, the loose clothes on his thin body, he looked like a Pierrot, his shoulders raised and hands folded before him, his long face tilted slightly, a mask of absolute repose. When Angela walked to him he didn't move, he stayed utterly still when she placed her finger on his forehead and down the stark line between his eyes, to soften the precise features of his carved face, to smudge the lines.

He was very talkative at dinner. She had never seen him so glib. Angela watched his beautiful hands and the drifting ashes. He sipped brandy and held it between himself and the candle and remembered his boyhood with a dramatic calm. He remembered the moments of delinquency and trespass and the early fraternal loves, dogs and boys and bicycles. He wasn't speaking to her, but to his own archives. Sometimes his eyes would pass through her and she was shocked by the contact with their flat white surface. When the bill came he paid it and gathered his car keys, wallet. He held the door for her, then brushed by. Angie was incidental, and central, extremely tired. She didn't know what to say, her untenable responses bleeding like dye into the parched space between them. But his impatience had nothing to do with her.

It was raining a little, so thoroughly *la nuit américaine*. Her red hair was spooled in the soft moist air. He gave her his arm, an old-world gesture, and Angie rested for a few minutes in this formality. They walked the freshly renovated riverbank, copper lamps through rain and foliage. He held her hand to lead her down the paved path beside the river. This posture evoked a girlishness in Angela, a Natalie Wood girlishness, and she tried to calm down. The lamps planted every few feet, their shadows loping from behind to ahead like fast solar transits.

The City Fathers had bestowed a marble bench where the path through the lamp-lit park concluded in an intimate amphitheatre, a stone slab like Tess's altar-tomb, quite dry. She leaned against it, her hands playing with pebbles produced somehow by this stone. Sam stood before her as if he would speak, his feet close together like a single narrow line of ink, impassive but formally perfect. He looked up. His glance strayed over her shoulder and then he looked into Angela's eyes. She had a glimpse of an alleyway, a long shadowed corridor in Sam's eyes before he looked away.

"Are you feeling all right?" She tried to touch him but he pulled back. "Are you angry?" she asked.

"Should I be?" He ran his thumb along her collarbone. Then he put his hand around her throat. He kissed her mouth while he squeezed her throat very slightly. She stopped standing and he supported her with his hand and his mouth. Then he was laughing, or something like it. His new ripple. "You're a mess," he said, and helped her up.

She backed away. "What's the matter?" he asked. She had a blank where her anger would be. Already, she'd forgotten and she accepted this as a remedy though she knew she would remember later, and often. If she just weren't so tired. He had kissed her too hard, it was nothing.

Fatigue had clawed many fresh lines in him. There was something new in his face, an absence of symmetry, mostly in the eyes; something had fallen from within. She touched his shoulder, and he flinched, an animal resisting the human touch, the domestication. He took her home and they slept in their separate places without malice; too old for malice.

Several days later he said he was feeling good again, only starved. Fine, he said, wincing when Angie tried to hold him. He needed to get some weight back. They went to many restaurants. They sat beneath the framed photographs of the city when it was frontier. They talked about their work. That is, Sam said the same thing over and over, looking carefully into Angela's cautious face: Ren really was the smartest guy around, wasn't he? Sam's real question poised like a stranger at the door. They ate. He remained very thin. And in the eyes, the reproach which he wouldn't name. Exhaustion, the corrupting alloy, seamed his face. They were both drinking a lot. Or maybe not. Only because they were out to dinner so often. They never drank during the day. They were thirsty. Angela touched her own skin for him, their eyes on each other, one apprehensive, the other amused in a way, a dry resolution of the doubt that once had made him ill. At night, after making love, and making love had become confident and bold, he would bring her ice water, standing above her in the half-tones of night. She learned to know him by the shining sound of ice.

Girls

It was raining so she took a cab from her office to the court-house.

"Wait a minute." She touched the cabby's shoulder and he jumped a mile. "Hold on. Please. Regina!"

The cabby looked pleased to see yet another fancy-dressed woman. He slowed into the curb, like he was expecting to have a good time. "That's her name?" he said. "Regina?"

"I know," said Angela. "And her middle name's Sunny."

Regina was wearing a chocolate-coloured trench coat. Her hair was damp and frizzy and the freckles sat like tiny stones under the rain on her face. She looked pretty and young. "Hello dog-face," she greeted Angie. She jumped into the back seat beside her. "Protecting the fake suede?"

"I don't like being wet in court."

The cabby looked into the rear mirror, catching Regina's eye.

"She can't help it," Regina told him. "Want me to drive? I'll drive if you want me to."

Angela was wearing a pale blue suede suit. Very light blue stockings. The blue shoes. She sat back, crossing her legs. "That's where you're going too, right?"

"Pre-trial. Second time we've scheduled. I hope he shows. The guy with the shoes." Regina looked at Angela's. "You'd like this guy."

"Yeah. Thanks. I love sleek little Italians with gold cuff links."

"Uh huh."

The cabby pulled up at the courthouse. Angela fished in her bag for a bill. He turned in his seat, looking like he wished they'd stay in there for the afternoon. Smiling. Angie put her hand on his sleeve and then said to Regina, "I'm going to kick butt today." Her breathy voice, low.

"Of course you are. What are you doing after you kick butt? Got time for a drink?"

"Anything. I just don't want to go home."

Regina was surprised.

"Is that awful?" Angela looked out the window. It was getting windy and grim.

"Sam's in bad shape, isn't he?"

"I need a break. Cut loose. What say we go out and do girl stuff." Angela's hand was still sitting on the cabby's arm.

Regina squinted at her. "Girl stuff?"

"Yeah. What girls do when men aren't watching."

Regina smiled. "Oh. Like drink and walk around in our bras and talk about oral sex."

"We'll go to my cabin and sit in the raw and make fun of my husband."

"We'll talk about the first time we did it."

"We'll fantasize about sexy cabbies."

"I love cabbies," said Regina, looking at him. He was young, looked like a student. "You're getting an MBA, right?"

"Fine arts," he said. He wore small frameless glasses, had shaved his head nearly bald. Angela touched his head. The guy pulled back. Regina looked at her, startled.

Angela's eyes were closed, and she was speaking very low.

"We'll confess to wanting to sleep with women, and laugh ourselves silly over the size of the average cock."

The cabby sat still.

"Pay the man, bitch," said Regina.

Angie took a ten and held it out to the cabby, tugging it a bit when he took it. "Keep the change," crooning. She slid over the seat and got out, then bent down and said, serious, low, "Thanks. I couldn't make it without you."

She and Regina walked toward the courthouse. Regina was shaking her head. "Aggressive, Ange. Funny."

Angela smiled.

"I'm not used to the barracuda routine." Regina was annoyed.

"That's your job."

"Right. Don't forget it. You're the sweet one."

They were standing in the drizzle. The wind was bad. Regina flicked at a water stain on Angela's jacket. "Come inside."

They went through the revolving doors, tall and heavy with brass handles, and stood in the cold foyer. It smelled of cigarettes. Everyone's voice echoed; it made things seem exciting and sad at the same time, like a train station.

"What's the matter with you and Sam?"

"It's nothing. He's in one of his I'm-going-bankrupt phases."

"Maybe he is."

"We've been here before."

Somebody tapped Regina on the shoulder and said, "I'm going out on a limb for you." He had draped a cashmere coat over his small shoulders. Angela looked down. The shoes were indeed impressive, tiny and soft as kid gloves. He held out his hand to her. "Well," he said, "don't tell me you're a legal beagle."

"This is my friend Angela, Tony. Don't feed her any crap, please. She will hurt you."

"Naw," said Tony. "Nice to meet you kid." He presented her with his card. "We need friends in this world."

"You're a consultant?"

"It's a loose description of what I do. It's just a starting point, Angie. Do they call you Angie?"

"C'mon Tony." Regina tugged his arm. "You've got a lady judge."

"You're a good girl," Tony said to her. Then he looked up at Angela. "You're a good girl, too. It's very nice you are a big woman. In Europe, the women are big. It's much better. They look after you good when they are big."

Pierrot

at night I dream of rivers

Sam sat on a stone fence beside the river. The fence was once a dike, a collection of cobbles; the pressure of the craftsman's hand still visible in the mortar, and you might imagine his confidence under the trees on a sunny afternoon, perhaps a summer day such as this, after the flood-waters had long receded, when the leaves blew out of a painting by Wyeth.

Sam's eyes were on the glitter of sun on water. Angela left the door open, her car leaning to the left where she pulled to the wrong side of the road. She heard the grasshoppers singing in the alfalfa, the purple flowers at the edges of her vision. She walked on the smooth, nearly tiled clay road. The sun was sweet with weeds, the breeze, heating and cooling and heating again.

"I saw you from the road," Angie said, relieved to see him out wandering. Lately, he'd been stuck like a train to its tracks, compelled by routine. "Out for a walk?"

His lips parted dryly, sand-coloured. "Yes," he said. He was shy, small, tentative.

"Come here often?"

"Why?"

"It was a joke."

"Oh. Oh, yes." He looked candid and uncertain.

Angie was thinking about dinner. Looked at her watch. She'd spent the day in the fictive measurement of billable hours. Sam's weird moods had put him on another calendar. She stood in her expensive office clothes, impatient and bored and uncomprehending, waiting for Sam to unravel. She was her dream-self, like a boy, or a clone of herself, asexual, a persistent little boy without innocence. She would try to be otherwise. Sam had journeyed to some desolate place of his own invention. He'd been gone a very long time.

That night they went driving. Sam was thin and unsteady on his feet but Angela was surprised nonetheless when he told her to drive. "Passive aggressive," she said, another joke, failed. They listened to Mahler, the low answering and slow acquisitions nearly too much. Sam staring ahead swayed a little with the motion of the music or the car. She glanced at him with what might pass for empathy. He looked like an old woman, the mouth full of pins.

"Do you mind if I turn this off?" she asked him. He said he hadn't noticed it was on. Angela asked again if she could do anything. Sam looked at her with the familial you-oughta-know, and she flushed.

Sam wanted to know about this boy who had killed the lawyer-woman. "He didn't kill her," she said. "Yeah right," Sam said, and Angela so mad she thought about sideswiping a telephone pole, maybe just take off the passenger side, wrap Sam in tin, the ultimate divorce. He said it was sickening, how could anyone be so vicious.

"How do you know so much about it?" she asked.

"I've seen enough," he said. "I wouldn't want to look at that sick stuff if I were you baby. Look at craziness, you get crazy. I'm just looking out for you. You don't know what you're getting into."

Angela was zealous over many things at once. It wasn't so uncommon, the combinations of death and sexuality, she said, and mentioned Freud, "and anyhow, Joey didn't do it, how could he, you should see him," she said, "and anyway Sam how do you know so much about what happened to Marlene?"

"I know a lot of things," he said, risking his life now.

They were driving briskly. Angela rarely looked at the road, more important than driving to get this straight, clear the air, question of priorities.

"Anyway," she said, "you're so smart, you know the cops have to get a conviction and it doesn't matter what the evidence is, they have to charge somebody. I think it's the worst kind of professionalism." She palmed the wheel and made a fast turn with great skill. "You seem to know a lot about this case," she said, "but I bet you don't know how the same cop fucked up the Northcott case in '88 because he took a statement without a lawyer and Northcott got off even though he for sure did it and now this cop is a sergeant till he gets a clear conviction so it doesn't matter how Joey's too small to punch a man as big as you, much less rape and cut a woman. The cops just need a fast conviction. And why the hell are we talking about this?"

He looked at her. Her words, like sea gulls desperate for scraps, flocked about till her hands were empty with testimony. In a low gentle voice, Sam said, "He's not even in a security prison, is he? When you see him, there isn't even a guard." He shrugged. "You're crazy."

Angela put her right arm over the seat, careful not to touch Sam. She steered with her knee and opened her window with the other hand. She would not be crazy. Besides, she suddenly realized what was bothering her. "How do you know what happened to Marlene Cook? I haven't shown you the file."

Sam had a secret, solemn and ingenious, Sam had a secret reverberant beyond his own telling. He should have been a lawyer, he could have been many things. "You have amazing instincts," she said. She looked at Sam, and he smiled wanly. "Oh baby, I do love you," she told him.

He sat back. Looked out the window. "But I'm not enough."

This, at last, feeling an edge in the quicksand.

"Nobody's enough for anybody."

"C'mon, Angie."

She tried again. "Sam, I'd like a child. I want some friends. I love my work."

He nodded.

"Why don't we?" she asked.

And again, Sam nodded. "We'll see," he said. "After you get finished with this boy. When you're not so busy."

They drove a while. Then Angela said, "Would you like to meet him?" When he didn't answer, she said again, "Would you like to meet Joey?"

Even in the tedious yellow streetlights, she could read Sam's unspoken response. Yes, he would meet the boy, if it would make her happy. And perhaps it would.

pushing against people with my hands on them

Angie met Regina and Patrick for a quick drink after work. Sam had gone to the coast for a couple of days. He looked better than he'd looked in weeks. It was a relief to be free of his sad watch-dog eyes. Regina and Patrick were great talkers. Regina found it endlessly funny that Patrick was a tennis instructor. She teased him for his good looks, called him a gigolo. Patrick laughed openly with her, revealing a modesty that Angie hadn't guessed was there.

They ordered tempura vegetables and another martini. The booze hit like sudden madness. By their third, they were super-stars and the bar was a warm audience. Angie, overcome by generosity, bought drinks for strangers and explained the vast similarities between tennis and law. She had a tendency toward analogy when the spirits were in her.

They had to go dancing. Regina took them to her favourite "meat market." "Ohhh, bad," said Angie, "gross expression." Disco never did go away. Vibes humming in her bones, Angie felt like disco was an old friend whom she'd never liked in the past but who compelled her with the longevity of the acquaintance and she danced herself to completion, they all did, formed a small circle, their faces very serious and devoted. Then they went to the place with good blues and billiard tables. They were only drinking beer by then. They all played brilliantly. And on the way home, they walked with their arms around each other and made ecstatic declarations of friendship. Simple as that. Forever. I love you guys. Me too.

They were cruising, Regina called it, cruising a downtown back lane trying to find their cars when they came across an office door open to a brightly lit room. They stopped, teetering, giggling, and peered around its iron frame, standing in the dust and dark seeking the magic of a stranger's privacy. It appeared to be the office of a graphic artist, the deep tilted desk, the bright lamps. On the walls, many photographs of landscapes. Patrick said, "Now isn't this nice," and stepped into the room. Regina and Angela gasped and laughed and followed till the three of them were abruptly sombre, looking at the photographs, wide silver portraits of water and land, the long arm of the river, and the water's reflection. The photographs had a gracious meditative quality, more rich than landscapes. The three drunken dancers had been found by beauty. They stood for perhaps a half-hour in the studio. Its owner never presented himself.

Somehow Angie drove home. It was utterly wonderful to find the house blank and empty. She sang as loud as she could, a bit of a medley, top of her lungs, wandered the house, wept over photographs, listened to Dylan, and with mature wisdom, drank several glasses of water. And then to bed, and alone, yes, no one about, bliss, unseen.

And then the back door shutting quietly. But by then, Angela was in a dreamless sleep.

May

Angela's mother leaned over the zinnias and she lifted their orange faces in her palm and said, "I'm totally gone on these things." She collected idiomatic expressions as if they were costume jewelry. Bent toward the flower garden in a violet dress, her white hair arranged loosely, she was vase-shaped, and softly melded with her surroundings. They murmured the names of perennials while Angela followed May around the flowers at a pace respondent to the delicate reach of their fragrance.

May served tea and this nearly appeased Angela's compulsions, though she knew she would go home and have a drink or two. For now, she pushed herself into the white wicker and cushions and focused hard to let the evening in. May put one claw hand over hers, trapping her, but said nothing, only tapping a rhythm strangely soothing as a lullaby without a melody. Angela withdrew her hand to scratch her leg. She wanted to replace it and did because May remained staring into nowhere, the piebald sunlight through the leaves.

When Angela agreed to stay for dinner it was past the time

when she would ordinarily be home to meet Sam who had returned from Vancouver that afternoon. When she phoned to tell him she would spend an evening with May, Sam left a gap like a bad edit in audiotape. Angela saw herself entering the house, she saw herself in the kitchen when he arrived, the smell of garlic and lemon and oil, she would stand in the white kitchen, harmonious, appropriate.

"I'm sorry to be such dull company." She dumbly watched her mother slice cucumbers.

May said, "Yes. You have always been dull. You were a dull child and now you are a dull adult." She placed a cucumber in Angela's mouth. "However you may keep me company at dinner because you have something to tell me. I want to know about this boy. But first, I want a drink."

"Thank god," said Angela. She wasn't released, but she would divert herself with relatively benign intoxicants. When she had the cork half-out she stopped and lit a cigarette. The wine glasses were green. She poured the wine and smoke into her. Fingers of liquor and cigarette smoke made points of light in Angela's blood, making her dizzy, an effect she liked. The edges of May's matronly figure were transfused with evening sun through the window.

Seated, the coherent shape of fork in her tuberous fist, May explained colour to Angela. Red, she said, is every colour but red. All the other colours in the spectrum are absorbed by the object we would call red. Except red. Red is really, she said, everything but red.

May's droll conversation that night only increased Angela's indiscriminate hunger. May expressed herself with a spacious candour, passionately noncommittal, like a teenager. She'd postponed self-definition, and this gave her the teenager's high morality, the subjunctive judiciary.

It made Angela thirsty. When she announced she would get another bottle of wine May nodded slightly and hacked the head off a spear of asparagus. Angela walked directly to May's bedroom, closed the door, sat near the pillow and dialled Patrick's number.

There would be a little time between leaving May's and being expected at home. She asked Patrick if he would meet her.

"Sure," he said, without much enthusiasm. "Everything all right?"

"Well I haven't sobered up yet, and I'm not going to, either. I'm not that dumb."

Patrick laughed and agreed.

Angela felt very light walking down the hallway toward the dining room. She stopped, leaning against the door frame as if in speculation. There was a black spot on the kitchen counter, looked like a bug, she leaned forward and put her finger on it, a bit of burnt food, oily. The kitchen gave onto the dining room. Her mother sat watching from her place at the table. Then like a breeze she felt Sam's eyes on her. She turned and he was standing behind the screen door. The surprise entered Angela thickly, a slow panic. But she was glad to see him.

"How long have you been standing there? May!" she called to her mother. "Sam's here! Well, come in my love. This is wonderful!"

"My love?" repeated Sam. He looked as if he didn't like the expression; she had never called him that before.

She was so glad to see him. He put his arm around her, or she tucked herself under him. She watched him take a handful of grapes. He sat down, tall and angular and crisp. In the fallen light she leaned toward him, fascinated by his snowy eyes. He was speaking with May, his face turned aside from Angela so the bones of his brow and cheekbone seemed to her refined as music on the page.

Between May and Sam there was an ambiguity that bordered on laughter, quizzical and insoluble, an unfinished joke. Angela, watching them over the years, had been reminded of dolphins. They were both, she decided, utterly foreign to her. This was her strength furthered by her study of law, to see clearly our estrangement from the people we love. For the first time that day, Angela relaxed, she swung her leg under the table, felt her contradictions of warm and cool skin, and in this placid form of auto-eroticism she dallied in Sam and May, her two most precious people, she swam in the temperate seas of their indifference.

Neither Sam nor May would ever speak of the other directly. They would allude to one another as if in speculation of their existence. When May said "Sam" she was saying, "If there really were a Sam." And Sam had often said of May, "She just doesn't seem like your mother." Still, this tentative rapport put them at ease; screened by their two-way mirrors, May and Sam were most free in mutual disbelief.

Angela imagined a time when she and her mother would speak directly about Sam. Just as May might one day speak of her own hungering marriage to Angela's father, enlisting Angie's errant womanhood in a final *rapprochement*. Angie would tell her mother how she loved Sam, how she felt starved by him. And May would take her side, a compassionate mother. This was just about as likely as Angie's childhood fantasy that when she died the gates would open in smoke and rapture and explanation.

Angela nurtured a supplement to the summer evening. She listened and contributed to the conversation, but like someone cupping a candle, she devoted herself to an impression of Patrick. Harmless as a stolen afternoon. It was not so much Patrick himself, nor Patrick the mirage, that counterfeit object of desire: it was Patrick as verb, as he existed in relation to Angela, an accompaniment, to draw her, to draw her out. Angela was clearly present in the conversation with her husband and her mother while the verb that was Patrick like a nonessential attribute enhanced her life. Angela was not duplicitous; she was multiple. And besides, it is perfectly normal to have a friend.

May planted her knotted fingers on the table and pushed herself erect. She lit a small lamp on the buffet and fetched the cigarettes. Under her throat the soft white skin in folds like rests from gravity. She had an affair with her own chronology but it was not intimate.

"I only fed you tonight because I thought you might have an interesting story," she told Angela. "You have not earned your supper."

Angela had never been any good at telling stories. Her skill lay in their destruction. When she prepared for a trial she constructed a bluff from which she released details like a fistful of fireflies. The audience in court was responsible for making up a moral tale, a plot with villains and victims.

She was overtaken by the cigarettes and the wine. The case was a sand dune. Her foot under the table searched for the brake. She put her hand on Sam's arm, beseeching. "Sam knows. Let Sam tell, " she said.

"I don't know anything about it," said Sam.

His disclaimer injected in her a mild toxin. "Oh but you do!" she said. "You were telling me the other night!"

He winced. She never wanted victory over Sam; she rushed to placate.

"He's been charged with second degree," she said. "They say he was alone but there was another boy with him. An older boy. It's all circumstantial. They found him in the house. Joey was standing at the door when the police arrived. It was like he needed them there. Like he was looking out for them. He had some things in his hands and a ring in his pocket. Marlene had some nice things, I imagine. It was a break and entry. Do you know what the cop said to me? He said, He's going to be charged with a B and E anyway, so what's the difference? Break and entry or murder. What's the difference?"

A boy would have no place there. He was too small, his small boy's hands, his skinny bones, the sternum apparent under his shirt, too small to touch the lean aging body. How stubborn and vain and self-denying Marlene had been to have remained so thin. Angela felt ashamed. "No one comes to see Joey. One cousin or aunt or something showed up and talked to him because the police made her but she really didn't know him."

"What about his mother?" asked May.

"She's a bitch," Angela said. "She's too fucking drunk and stupid to look after her own kid."

May put out her cigarette with tolerant weary grace.

"He's not a kid. He's been transferred. His case is in adult court," said Sam, cool, lips unmoving, like a ventriloquist.

She'd intended to tell him this eventually, workday news taken home. But he already knew. She had a lousy memory. But how could she remember the future? She rubbed at her forehead as if she would erase consciousness.

"No one seems to know him," she said, rubbing. "He's an odd boy. I don't understand why they've transferred."

She wanted plainsong. She wanted to go home. She rose to go. The wind had picked up and then it began to rain in thick silver waves. May and Sam and Angela stood at the front door behind the screen and felt the blowing rain.

Across the street someone opened a door and let out a little boy. He was perhaps three years old and stark naked. He ran down the steps and danced in the rain, waving his skinny arms, lifting his limbs. His white bum shone in the light. He saw them watching and threw his celebrant arms in the rain. When he waved, the palms of his hands like the white soles of his feet were pale as the undersides of a small mushroom, his white palms and his white tail dancing in the forests of the night.

dancing on the bones

The streets were wide and glossy with rain. She followed his headlights home. She followed him home as if the distance between them were something chronic and inconsolable. He went directly to bed and she followed him there and lay in their bed like smoke or cream and spoke of his work and his troubles in a voice so soft as to be nearly unvoiced. When she touched him he had flown from her. She was captivated, tracing him like a vapour trail. In this penumbral state she fell asleep.

She was asleep when she felt him arrange her limbs and open her legs and enter her, riding her back. She was so wet she thought she would drown them both. Then he began to knead her with his fists between her shoulder blades, the pain from this transfused itself through Angela to Sam and with the fingers of one hand he pried her open wide, wide, she was open too wide, he would sink inside her and she pulled herself closed. Then his hand was a talon in the flesh either side of her spine lifting her. She met the pain of his claws with reciprocal pain because she wore her claws inside. They met this way, pain to pain. Above the house above the trees over the river he flew away with her.

Sharon

The river cut into its banks, escarped the mud to form steep cliffs that looked like tooth fillings; at its edges the thick black gumbo dried into white clay. The boat churned up muddy water and left a wake shaped like the formations of geese. It was fall. They had passed through the city while the company was still noisy with gin. The women wore white shoes and everyone proved their love for a home town by naming buildings from the river, their secret side hidden by gold elm leaves.

They cruised out beyond the floodway, willows a soft milky grey flood-twisted on the modest riverbank, long rectangular farmland worked even to the combed soil between planted windbreaks. They were amazed by the heat, their shoes removed now and still a sun-glow in the skin beneath summer dresses. Sharon and Regina and Angela with Sam. Where heat would come with such intensity as if it were generated from the earth.

They saw, white as chrome beside a red barn, a water tower so shiny it strobed their eyes. A man stood on a scaffold repairing the tower. Sam looked at him, isolated, far away, and he said, "What a lucky guy." It looked as if the man were painting the dome of a cathedral. Sam throttled down and Sharon stumbled. Everyone reached up to save her. Rocked by their own waves they circled her, a compass around the pole. Sharon's hand was on her belly.

It clouded over on the way back to the city, and the women put on sweaters but Sam remained bare-chested. Wind whipped their hair in their mouths and eyes. The boat was something brittle and unmade for water, stunned on impact. When Sam yawned, his large mouth revealed stained teeth, gold-filled. He was chilled, his skin tight and white and cold. Angela wondered how he could be casual with his own flesh. It was too noisy to shout. They pushed their faces into the wind.

They had taken three hours to drift out of the city but they were back downtown in twenty minutes. Regina had to go to her office. They moored at a shipping dock high above the water so their lines wouldn't reach the cleats. Sharon fit her fingers between the boards, her hand slipping into the black wet space, the green shine of algae and wood engraved in red. It would soon rain. The air smelled of scared-up dust. They heaved Regina from gunnel to dock, palmed her laughing.

Regina grinned down at them, collecting her basket and a bag of coarse late-summer fruit stained precisely in the shape of a pit. Angela balanced on her toes to see her friend. It was the rocking of the boat or regret for the passage of a day made her stomach fall. Everything suddenly grey. A concrete parking lot and ugly new stucco warehouses had displaced the old red-brick waterfront.

Regina crouched down to Angie. "Sam seems OK," she said to her.

"Today was a bit better." Angela said this quickly, quietly.

Then while she and Regina said their amiable goodbyes and Regina turned toward her car, Angela called out. They hadn't been aware of five boys idling on the timber, smoking and watching. Regina hesitated and then stuck out her tongue. They squinted at her sceptically, but one boy suddenly smiled. Sharon stood on the bow, a frowzy abstracted woman on an expensive boat. Her other hand caressed, her new habit, smoothed her belly.

Sharon was four months pregnant. The father was, she said, "presumably male." She offered no further details. She said only that she was "of an age," and told Regina and Angela that they could have been the father but they were too much like women. "And Sam," she said, looking at him, "Sam's too territorial." Sharon was suspicious of civil contracts, and was adamant, it was no one's business but her own. A child without encroachment. Sharon's child, wholly.

Angela felt betrayed and envious. She wouldn't look at Sharon, would look, avoid her eyes, stare at the secretive belly, embarrassed by her covetous eager curiosity. She wanted to ask Sharon what it felt like, but something stopped her. Regina had no such scruples, so Angela became a voyeur to their gossip. She camouflaged her resentment with gifts for the baby.

They had settled into a new phase of their friendship, and Sharon's transformation had almost made them into a family, with a family's unspoken scandals and tolerance and a kind of sloppiness that comes with long-standing intimacy. Sharon and Sam and Angela went out for Chinese food on their way home. Sharon sat beside Sam, and when she put her hands on his face and kissed him, she tucked her chin in so her neck formed slack folds. It was unmistakable, a sister's kiss. Then she looked at Angela, a clear conscience and a stolid form of parody in Sharon's eyes.

full of warmth touching these strangers in my life

Joey's boredom was a thistle, a successful contagion in the detention centre where he now lived. The food was good and he had grown nearly three inches since his incarceration six months ago. Outside, a construction crew was hammering the fresh foundation of a new wing. The boys were awakened by the jackhammers and pile drivers and the high-pitched signals of trucks backing up, the mechanical bones of backhoe, caterpillar, orange as the fall pumpkins, redolent of diesel fuel and loudly stimulated by a generator. Coming at dawn the noise was subliminal and the boys had woken with it as they had woken into their starved lives, as if the denial of bread and love were their own responsibility, as obvious as the size of their feet or the shape of their ears.

At two o'clock Joey was seated on the third stair from the top, in his long-thumbed hands a slinky-toy. He was having a complicated race with another inmate who had a small dense rubber ball. The loosely defined and unspoken object of the game was to match the ascent and descent and ascent and descent of the ball with a single descent of Joey's slinky-toy. Neither boy spoke more than the singular Fuck when the game went awry. When the spring coil made it downstairs and the ball had achieved two complete throws, Joey slid down a step or two and his companion fingered the spring coil and lifted it to him like he had a trout by its gills. Their unintentional plan was to persist with the sallow rhythms of this game until 5:30 when they were permitted to turn on the television. It was a cool day and they were glad to be inside.

Joey had grown. He was the star basketball player of the youth centre. He would never be tall but his torso had thickened. His legs were pistons and he was fast on his feet. He played with an insouciance intended to disguise his excitement; too competitive to reveal his competitive spirit.

In a cage as bland as the youth detention centre, in a city defined by a tough climate, zoned for malls dulled by muzak, infinite Barbara Streisand, there's nothing beyond, everything is duplicated and franchised, the cage that makes cage. But Angela, entering this sanctum, vespertine, sweet relief from daylight, admired his long black hair grown into a ponytail and she knew instinctively that her client had found in the rituals of detention that long-denied maternal rhythm which rooted his spidery roots and his weedy growth; he was grounded as he'd never been in his life. He'd found an edge and while there were, beyond, close as tomorrow, other edges, he was resting here, he was growing.

He was a young man. His eyes retained their incurious glaze but he was nearly full-sized. Regular food, regular bells, regulations, had finally rocked him into maturity sufficient to place him in much greater jeopardy. When Angela went to see him, she saw what the court would see, that Joey looked big enough for the rational acts of rape and murder.

They had a wonderful visit. Joey was so improved that Angela was happy as a Sunday-school teacher. She could support him unfailingly. The yellow visiting room smelled of boiled short ribs and fat, grey foam rising in the water, broth like bile, the cremation smell. "It's a shame," she said, "we can't go out and eat in a restaurant." *Restaurant* floated like the icon of a mysterious tribe, evoking in Angela the relief of Béarnaise and white linen, and in Joey the deafness of someone listening to a foreign language.

He hid his feet between desiccated cushions the colour of goat's cheese. His short legs folded under his womanly buttocks and his wrists rested between his knees so the hands curled childishly as if they would cling to the vacant nourishment of the TV. She didn't turn it off though she did turn it down but Joey didn't notice because he never listened to the words. The images blinking by appeased him, eye to nictitating eye, the pap, the television. For the first time she noticed that his hair as it was parted from a white vein dividing the hemispheres of his head formed a chevron, a widow's peak on his high forehead, and upon this peak, the baby-fine hair whirled, a hazy star.

Angela nearly knew the circumstances that had brought Joey to this place. When Joey was little not so long ago he fell out of the arms of his foster family and into the chalk-circle of a burglary ring. He was the youngest and the most advantageously under-nourished and the Fagan was not much older but much bigger.

"He was a really nice guy. When you didn't make him mad he was a very OK guy," Joey said. Though his transmission failed while the commercials were on, he proved to be a storyteller of sensitivity. And that is how Angela learned, Joey had a murmuring of intelligence, a vestigial muscle that gave him the ability to entertain. What he lacked in penetration he made up for in his undifferentiated appreciation for the non-caste characters, the untouchable limbs of his tale.

Since he was the smallest boy Joey went in first through an open window or through the pet door. He was always teased when it was the pet door. Then he would open the place to his friends and they wouldn't have to break anything or cause any damage. On the night when the lady was hurt, everybody was in a lousy mood. They'd been staying at the fair where maybe the fries were rancid. Angela was surprised to hear the word *rancid* coming from Joey, and she began to warm to the doubling within Joey's vocabulary, which had up till then been like debris. Anyway, chocolate makes me, Joey said, antsy. So when Lewis started razzing, Joey lost his cool. He climbed up big Lewis and choked him at his throat and everybody had to pull him off. "I was like a cat on him," Joey said laughing. Angela laughed too.

The lady had a carving, a lot of them, on a round table where the green light was. Really weird. Joey looked from the screen to Angela, in his brown eyes the wonder of stone.

Other things, many things, strange in the lady's house. Lights over pictures. There was this table desk with feet like lions' feet. She has or she *had* a thing for cats because every picture had a cat in it and on this one place a bunch of black cats out of some black rock. That was (and Joey ravening his mind for the word) beautiful. She even had a piano. Rich.

Lewis gets mad. He starts singing this song from Aerosmith, "Eat the Rich." Joey said the word *eat;* Angela saw his perfect teeth. She smiled, an indulgent and trustworthy aunt. "But I go, Shut up Lewis. Whispering. But Lewis he starts singing louder and louder. Lewis is singing real loud, he's like a rock singer, he's yelling. Christ, it scared the f, the f, the friggin wits out of me."

Angela sat like a child opening Christmas presents.

"So all friggin Cain breaks loose."

Oh Joey, Angela opening yet another present; your father said Cain, the mildew of residential schools.

"Yeah it was bedlam, nutso, completely. Lewis, he picks up this lady's shoe and he starts using it like it's a mike. And with his arm he's swinging around playing the guitar like you know. Singing. And you know what that's like."

Angela nodded and then said, "Not exactly." She liked it when Joey translated for her. "Rock singer," his curved syllables, and "bedlam," somewhere a Scottish minister kindly and prosaic. Joey governed his story, speaking gently in his several translations, and Angela wanted to intensify the effect. "Like MTV," Joey said. He looked at her with patience.

Now he watched her while he talked. When Angela recalled the scene, so many times and often unbidden, she would see the rich light thrown from a brass lamp, heavy framed photographs and the incongruity of white lace, silver cutlery, the carved furniture. She saw Marlene, a wispy figure at the top of the stairs. Marlene would have been visible from the foyer where Lewis was pulling the drawers from their casements; then she withdrew but not before Lewis had looked, sensing, the last edge of her nightgown as she retreated to her bedroom to call the police. Angela could not remember Joey's words though she heard Marlene's chipped voice and saw the black lines of panic, the jigsaw of Joey's story. These things were audible in a memory that Angela's body stored beneath her ribs. And the rest, Lewis running upstairs, how he took the stairs so fast he clawed the wallpaper and what happened up there, in Marlene's bedroom.

Then Joey, abruptly silent, the oracle in retreat. There was no reason for this, other than the impulse to deny himself the rightful plunder of an entertainer. The geriatric smells resumed, took their place on the palate. His neck was turned at an impossible angle. Body, boxed and muscular, fixed to the TV, large head and its brown eyes directed at Angela seated beside him. That masculine smell mixed with food. Where did you go when Lewis ran upstairs? I went up too. What did you do there? I saw him. Did you touch her? Lewis tied the nightgown around her throat. What did you do? I saw. Then he smiled shyly, because to their minds, the naked body would come warm and from another story, alluring. Angela looked from his eyes to his narrow mouth and a smile neat as bone.

Somebody knocked and told Angela that she had a visitor. Angela said, Just a minute, not looking away from Joey's eyes. What did Lewis do? He hit her with something. Like maybe an ashtray. Again and again many times. And he choked her too. And then Lewis raped her. Joey's voice was bevelled so each sentence rode a burnished and boyish surface and concluded with a lip like a question mark. It was a beautiful voice. His words were transcribed to innocence by her listening.

Again they were interrupted by staff reminding Angela with more urgency, someone had to speak with her. Angela nodded, distracted.

Joey's eyes on her and he said, "She didn't look at me though. I don't know where I was or if I was in the room or if I only heard it and saw what I heard."

Angela saw Joey curled up, the small boy he was then, outside the bedroom, in a corner with his face pressed against his knees.

"What about the blood?" he said then. "How come you never ask me about the blood, how it never got on me?" Angela looked at Joey's hands clutched to his pant legs.

But the staff would wait no longer. Angela really must come. They clucked with impatience and looked disapproving as she passed by them through the narrow hall. Joey turned up the volume on the set; she could hear it on her way to the kitchen. And there, seated at the table like an itinerant doctor, was Sam.

Before him lay the staples of breakfasts and lunches, peanut butter, mayonnaise, a vat of margarine, a loaf of bread leaning from a plastic bag, darkly congealed jam on the table. He wore a dove-grey suit, a silk-wool blend, Angela nearly drunk on the richness of the fabric, the watery complex of grey with blue silk threads and the firm white shirt as it framed his jaw. He had placed his chair sideways to the table and crossed his legs, casual, pensive, elegant, clearing a space between himself and the mess, as was his privilege.

"Is everything all right?" Angela stopped before him, truant.

"Randy had to tell me where you were."

"Sorry," she said. She looked at the floor. Then her anger rose up, and the familiar feeling of quicksand. "I'm working," she said.

He shook his head.

"Goddamn you. Enough. I'm working. I can't always call you first."

He was waiting for her to start making sense.

"No," she said. "Stop doing this. You're like a cop. Don't do this. You're losing me."

"Oh," said Sam, recognizing English. "I know."

Her hands were shaking, she reached for him. "Come and meet him." She pulled at his sleeve, begging, brought him to his feet. "Come, please, I'll introduce you to Joey."

To her surprise, Sam complied. In her shaking hand, she held Sam, compelled him to the TV room where Joey sat on the couch, lanky and bored. He'd put on a baseball cap backwards. "Joey," she said, beginning. But Sam had breezed by and stood over the boy.   .

Sam's voice was jocular. "Joey!" he said offering his hand.

Joey shook Sam's hand, reluctant.

"How's it going?" Sam asked.

"OK, I guess."

"I hear you're a pretty good basketball player," said Sam.

"Yeah." Joey waited for the man to go away. He looked at Angela. He was patient only for her.

"This is Sam," Angela said. "My husband."

Joey showed more interest, took a fast look at Sam's clothes. Angela was again aware of how inexplicable Sam could be. She sat down, buying time. Forced herself to be calm. "Have a seat, Sam." He did. She felt tender toward him then, his terrible vulnerability. "Joey was telling me exactly what happened the night at Marlene's house." Joey looked at Sam as if Sam had already heard he wasn't the guy who did it. The atmosphere improved; Joey assumed that Sam was on his side, too.

"Are you a lawyer like her?" Joey asked Sam.

"No," said Sam. "I'm in business."

Joey nodded. Then, slyly, teasing, "You got a pretty wife."

Angela said, "That's enough!" and Sam smiled. "Thank you," he said. "She talks about you a lot."

Joey looked at her, trust and affection she'd never seen in him before. She said, "Joey's a great kid. Everything's going to be fine."

Joey was so invigorated, he walked them to the door. He wanted to shake Sam's hand again. "Come back soon," he said. Angela laughed. The nicety sounded funny in him.

Sam and Angela walked to their separate cars as if they'd been visiting family. When Sam turned to tell her that he would see her later, he was going to the office for a while, he had tears in his eyes, his brittle chilled exterior and this suffusion of tears clear in his unreddened eyes.

The Show

The gallery had curated a major retrospective of May's work. When they had first broached the subject with her, May had said, "But I'm not dead yet!" The procedure was long and difficult and May often remarked that it was not so much an exhibition as an open coffin. The ironic and collateral distance from herself had folded like a pleat in fabric and she was at last in descent from her own simple mortal origin. It was like watching a photograph come into focus, the black branches of a winter tree.

"She's been run down by all these images of herself," Angela said to Sam. "She used to be so flexible. Now she's stiff. Like she's stationary." Angela looked at Sam's sad Pierrot posture, and laughed a little. "Runs in the family," she said. "She doesn't even laugh anymore."

"I heard her laughing. Wasn't that her you were talking to last night?" said Sam.

Angie looked hard at him a moment. "Yes, Sam. That was her." She pushed her hair from her forehead. "Tired. Are you?"

"No."

"What's work like these days?"

"There isn't any."

She heard him. Nodded. "It'll get better," she said.

Sam said, "No, Angie. I think I'm going under."

"You've said that lots of times."

"This time it's really bad."

"Then let's get rid of it all. Let's get out." Angela held her hands palms up, her common gesture, emptying her pockets.

"You don't know anything," he said. Sam always stood apart from her now, where he could see her clearly.

Suddenly angry, she took a glass of champagne from a passing tray, and said, "I can't wait for this thing to be over."

Angela had devised a distracted air, the bland virtue of a hyperactive child playing quietly with a puzzle. Tonight, she held her face open and complaisant, in defence, to remove herself from implication. She said, "I'm happy for her, I really am. I just want my mother back."

May approached, and Sam kissed her. May was short of breath. She was wearing too much rouge. Cobalt eye shadow in her tear duct. She clutched her knotted hands before her and said nothing, smiling politely as if they were all strangers.

The gallery began to fill with people, an occasion for chic. It was immense, four large rooms and a bare wood floor, party noise resounding, loud enough for secrecy and so crowded it was private. Intimate, they shouted, they held each other like megaphones, amplified and witty.

Angela drank champagne and watched her mother eddy through the crowd, their blandishments falling from her thin shoulders. Sam stayed at May's side. Angela tried to speak to them once but May had resigned herself to yet another torrent of praise. Sam looked at Angie, unspoken, Why have you come?

Angela drifted over to commiserate with one of May's atypical acrylics from the late seventies. A blonde in a white bathing suit beside a swimming pool in May's favoured colours, a palm tree, a tan, the woman's perfect legs curved beneath her so the lean calves, her breasts, the slightly muscular health, her head thrown back, expressed an extraordinary and contemporary beauty. After two column-inches of hesitation, the critics had declared it "ambiguous," their highest praise. Angela, looking now at the magazine style, its relentless finish, marvelled again over her mother's control. The ambiguity was not in the painting but in its viewer. How could anyone accept such flat superficiality without seeking an edge or a tear in the canvas? The painting was seamless. The gap resided in the gallery, in the educated guess.

People didn't stay long. They lit the rooms with the astonishment of their own beauty and then withdrew. Sharon remained with Sam and Angela and May. And surrounding Sharon, a collection of men. The pregnancy had softened Sharon's features and rounded her body; the modest tilt of her spine was a signal of girlhood and maternity, innocence and wisdom. She had exchanged the suits for paisley cotton skirts from India, and she embellished her new figure with a mix of stockings and woollen gloves, patterned scarves and embroidered vests. It was camouflage through an overwhelming of the senses, an excess of visual information behind which her belly grew. She had never looked more beautiful. The men devoted to her their respectful and ardent attention. They employed the space of the gallery to view her from its several vantages, their postures full of patient and gentle strength.

Since the fourth month when the baby began to move, Sharon's independence had become polyandrous. By choosing no husband, all men had become husband and all men fathers. By virtue of a wonderful amnesia, the lost paternity of the child transcended genealogy. Even Sam seemed to forget. He was gallant and impeccable.

At two a.m., May was suddenly young. She invited everyone to her home, her vitality a night-light making children of them all. May sat on the floor, the room illuminated softly, their faces handsome and attentive to their own divestment. She held her hands up for them to see. "Aren't ruins more beautiful than youth?" she asked.

They told small mysteries till dawn. And from their brief respite, they drove away through green transparent streets. Sharon chose to sleep in May's guestroom. When Angela turned to say goodbye from Sam's car, she saw the two women with their arms around one another and she thought, now we have abandoned our beginnings everything is possible. Even this strange twinning.

At the Park

Sharon was now so pregnant she walked like she was holding a beachball between her knees. She ground down the heels of her sturdy white sandals, and waddled, splayed, puffing. Regina walked behind making duck noises. Angela dreaded Regina's departure that afternoon. It had been OK while the three of them were together. Regina deflected the weird energy between Angela and Sharon. Regina deflected everything, that was her style, made it easy to be with her, nothing going to happen, not in any serious way. Regina had mastered the art of rolling a stone, the way she always undermined you, mocked you, teased you while she loved you. That day, she was a buffer between Angela and Sharon, between whom the tension had been growing with the size of Sharon's belly.

They were both tall women, Sharon and Angela. Sharon had been square in shape before she had grown her maternal silhouette. Her jaw was the box upon which her square face sat, her neck a cylindrical connector to her torso and sturdy legs. She had, however, the nicest feet. Square-toed, pudgy, affectionate feet. Angela, on the other hand, plump and dimpled everywhere as if virginal, the creamy flesh, coals glowing within, sweetly scented, warm-blooded. But today Angela was diminished by Sharon's annunciation. She felt scrawny and polluted by coffee and car fumes and pesticides. Common. Sharon's was the purified plentiful body, Sharon's was ample and yielding. She wore a maternity dress the colour of salmon as if she would also steal the hues from Angela's palette.

They went to the zoo, had lunch at the conservatory, walked through the park, and threw pennies at the statue of the pissing Blue Boy. In these last weeks of Sharon's pregnancy she was inexhaustible, emphatic and demanding. Glorious, aglow, and absorbed, her body the sole event on the planet, her belly the matrix for all creation. She was insistent that her two friends share in the miracle of her profusion. Every topic was, in its essence, childbirth: food, law, love, politics, shopping, the environment, the future, the past, the moment, all.

And her friends did participate. Regina, who had chosen a tubal ligation when she was thirty-three, particularly enjoyed Sharon's pregnancy, wondered obediently whether the moraine in the landscape of Sharon's belly was an elbow or a knee. She paid close attention to Sharon's diet and laughed with delight over the elastic in the waistband of Sharon's new jeans. She watched over the maternity like a movie reviewer at a film festival. She turned to Angie, winked, whispered, pointing at Sharon, "She thinks she's doing it with her brain."

Then Regina went home, and left Angela all alone with the Madonna.

What gave Sharon the right to magnanimity? It was not by any act of creative will, the child developing left-handed and musical in its third trimester. Why had Sharon so gained in stature? Pounds and pounds of stature. They walked silently across the clover while a jet scarred the sky, a sound that always filled Angela with aching loneliness. Sharon put her arm around Angela while they walked. It gave Angela a crick in her neck. Bloody heavy arm. The grass was shrill in the heat. They approached one of the innumerable flower beds, geraniums, petunias, trite as a garage sale, flowers like the flag, red and white.

Even the parturient Sharon could not resist trying to break through Angela's cranky silence. "How's it going?" she asked.

Angie relaxed a bit under Sharon's hand. "Not so good. It's wearing me out."

"The Joey case."

"Yeah."

"Must be distressing. A young kid like that."

"Well he's just so sort of undeveloped. Young for his age. Stunted. Fucked up. It's not fair."

They stood still. Sharon crossed her arms across the table of her belly, a posture that divided her pregnant body from her thinking head. "Stunted," she said.

"Little. Unfed. Really small. Or, like he was before he was arrested. Now he's growing like a weed."

"But he was little when he did it? Or, like, didn't do it?"

"A dwarf. Little. Piddly. Didn't grow. Not before now."

"And this was a really violent attack?"

Angela wondered how she'd tell Sharon she wanted to go home. "Really," she said. "Really, yeah. Big time. Sickening."

"So point it out. Little boy, big crime. You know Angie, you should get a splatter expert. Get in some expert." Sharon was getting excited, on a holiday from her body. "Get in some expensive splatter expert. American. They love American experts. Get him to measure the blood at the scene, and measure the blood on the boy. Show up the difference, right? Small boy, big blood."

Angela studied Sharon's shadow. It was the most beautiful shape, like a bleeding heart, how beautiful and lush and full. She ran her eyes over the heavy curves of Sharon's body, greedy for the pain it gave her. Then a frisbee nearly sliced the scalp from their skulls. They laughed and ducked. A group of kids at a birthday party. "Bunch of bad apples," said Sharon, affection for the entire world catching in her throat.

Act 5

In the courtroom Angela's metabolism idled high, the exertion shining her body with a salty wash. She liked litigation best, preferring the collective fantasy and her role as ingénue.

On the first day of Joey's trial she moved about Sam's house like a camera without film, glossing, thoughtless. She showered and dressed and performed the routine of morning. When she was spoken to she gave a rapt show of attention and no response. She had been awake for three days following the night of May's retrospective, transported by coffee and Scotch.

She sustained this acceleration for the two weeks of the trial. She approached the witnesses as if she were passing them in the park, casually, caressing the crowd with her voice. She was detached, that was the most destructive thing. Undisturbed by their statements to the Crown, her placid scepticism emptied every statement. She displaced their testimony with doubt, with alternative versions of the events. Each time the Crown would sew shut a passage of Joey's confession, she'd rip it open, lucid and gentle, willing to spare everyone's feelings. She moved because she enjoyed motion. Late in the second week, the Crown counsel resorted to a parody of Angela's gestures. That's when she knew she'd won.

Her devotion was ruthless. She worked very late and ate with the other lawyers or alone in her office. The fatigue didn't catch her face, she passed through so smoothly. She dressed with faultless taste, not a line out of place. Never had she been more narrowly focused, more blissfully engaged. She had no other interest and was like a mother in her sanctified absorption. All was law, all was the destruction of the Crown's argument, all was Joey's trial. One day she arranged her many shoes in alphabetical order in the walk-in closet, her typographical imagination a visual mystery. And the last leaves fell unregarded in the garden.

In her three or four hours of sleep, Angela's shallow breathing like the slender undulations in prairie, she dreamed, if she dreamed at all, of snow between harrow lines, powder on the porous flesh of land, cloudy skies and white fields. In sleep, she longed for winter and flung her arms above her head, clutched her white hands together, an alabaster body perfectly complete.

In her professional ecstasy, she forgot to touch Sam. Her untouched body had its sole contact with Joey, whom she soothed with a mother's chastity, his shoulder, his rumpled hair, closely speaking into his ear her comfort and her advice. Again and again, until it didn't matter if her eyes were opened or closed in sleep, it was Joey's quizzical face she saw, her sole responsibility. She spoke to him privately in the crowded courtroom, looking down his young neck into the shirt collar, placing her hand on his arm to efface the tension she felt and hated in him, positioning herself between Joey and the technical game of the trial.

It felt self-destructive to leave Joey in custody each evening. She went back to her office to study her notes for hours after adjournment, had a drink there and worked, and waited for him to reappear and breathe air into the texts and transcriptions. She would get him off. The courtroom filled her with an echoing vanity as she ran over in her mind her daily successes which she read in the approving eyes of the judge and the sympathetic laughter from the observers when she spoke with humour, unerringly perceptive, an expert of the surprise angle. She felt kindly toward the Crown counsel, her Learned Friend, and laughed at his stiff jokes. She was more articulate than she'd ever been in her life. Images filled her speech, hyperbolic and magical.

In her professional life Angela had learned with a conviction normally attributed to prejudice to associate communication with transgression. Real thinking, real being, she thought, is by definition transgressive. She was constructing a visionary case for Joey, one that linked the material with the immaterial, a contradictory dynamic, gyroscopic and perpetual and, once it was instilled in the judge's mind, indelible. There was nothing to do but hover over the work until her presence would no longer be needed and it would run forever like a machine that runs on truth.

It was a question of timing. How could little Joey commit violence on a grown woman? She called witnesses who spoke of him as a child, his aunt, his teachers. Despite their sketchy knowledge of his interior life they could eagerly testify that he had always been scrawny. Angela's ersatz dialogue erased the presence of tall muscular Joey so completely that the audience stopped staring at him. He'd dissolved into the blank space normally assigned to victims. Joey didn't notice. He didn't notice much. He was forbearing. As if he were awake during open-heart surgery. Leave it to the pros.

He would survive the trial through dormancy, a hibernation. His figure in the courtroom was a decoy. Joey was elsewhere. Angela knew him to be in hiding and she devoted her own pulse to supplement his, seated beside him, her glance fetching him, her emphatic presence meant to inform him as an act of faith during his absence. Joey was motionless, blended, something in him withheld. It made her ache for him, that he should know so much about protective camouflage and have such control over his fear. "What do you hope for?" she asked. "You said you'd buy me a basketball," he said, and smiled into his collar, impish, so no one could see.

During the Crown's examination Angela was in the habit of studying her fingers upon her pen. On the tenth day she looked around and for the first time in weeks brought the erratic world into focus. The observers of the trial were like tertiary actors, next to the press, next to the legal teams, like a Greek chorus. But Patrick was from another lifetime, and she couldn't place him at first, had a dizzy notion he was from her family. Sitting beside Patrick was Sam, the two men in identical postures, left leg over right. Patrick sat very still, watching Joey with calm compassion. Sam's eyes were on Angela and when she looked up he raised his eyebrows and smiled, a wary conspirator, a tight spotlight pinning her to a small place on stage. His hatred exposed the bones of her face and she was aware of the teeth in her jaw, the strong cartilage attached to her skull. She felt responsible for the tissue and muscle, the person created through appetite and instinct. With his eyes still on Angie, Sam leaned toward Patrick and spoke in his ear. Perhaps he was imitating the way she spoke to Joey. She saw the courtroom as a cell dividing.

She had to cross-examine the cop who had made the initial report on entering Marlene's house. She was acutely aware of her back or the entire shape of herself cut out from the estranged atmosphere. She brought the words forth from the base of her spine, her bowels. The problem was the pet door. Three times, she asked the cop how he had come to the conclusion that the tampering had been *recent.* "Was it a fresh wound?" she asked, to the amusement of the audience. But she was distracted and she didn't hear his response. Her mouth filled with acid. She asked for a recess.

When she looked next, Patrick and Sam were gone.

Late afternoon and already the streetlights were overtaking daylight. She walked quickly, so the black robes opened either side, revealing her long legs. Her red hair fell over her shoulders. Beneath the robes, she wore a grey suit, the stockings, her high heels. She nodded to people. She walked her thoroughbred walk down the carpeted hallway from the courtroom. She opened a small door to her left, and disappeared. She was always doing that. Disappearing.

colouring outside the lines

She arrived home late. It had been a big strategic error, losing the significance of the pet door because she had let herself be distracted by Sam and Patrick. She planned to revive the point tomorrow but that would be hard to orchestrate, especially now that the Crown had seen her hand. The point was intended to be climactic; in the morning it would be merely initiatory.

The house was in darkness but he was sitting outside. She knew it unerringly when she arrived. She didn't go in but walked around to the back where he was sitting on the deck, very straight in his chair. Her longing felt like fear when Sam turned to switch on a lamp and she saw his calm white face.

He would obviously never speak. Angela said, "It didn't go very well today."

Sam studied her as if she had given a pseudonym.

"I wasn't very polished," she persisted. "I missed my chance. Tomorrow I'll catch up. I've got to."

He smiled very briefly. She knelt beside him, and then she said, "You were with Patrick."

"An accident."

If she spoke now she would illustrate a story she didn't know she'd told. They looked at each other with curiosity.

"Sam, I wish I could make you happy."

Sam saw that she was still in court, the efficient professional, and it was true to her lawyer's intuition to shift the premise when she didn't like a consequence. She spoke from a place beyond him, letting down the words in a womanly voice. And she didn't touch him.

"Do you still love me?" she asked, her catechism. He said that he did. There was nothing else to say. She went to their room to change.

She stepped by memory to the loft, feeling the stairs. Except for the wedge of yard-light, the bedroom was in darkness. But through the white screen, a lamp in her office, soft as a night watch in a sickroom. She had left a light on in the early morning. It had been a cold pleasant morning at 6:30 when she began to work. Sam had already gone, so she worked while she was still in bed in her glasses and her socks, blissfully unperceived. She had celebrated Sam's absence with a bit of Kahlúa in her coffee and told herself it was compensation and if this were melancholy she liked it in small doses.

She was unzipping her skirt as she walked in the light thrown from the other room and stepped out of her clothes into her office where the desk lamp shone. Her desk was a raft and the single thing she owned in Sam's house. Every drawer to her desk was opened. She went to close them. In her chest the self-reproach, a small anxiety. The bottom drawer contained personal letters. Old things. The binder was red, she thought, and beneath it, a blue notebook, miscellaneous and sentimental. She thought the binder on top was red but she couldn't be sure. She closed everything carefully with the tips of her fingers.

She went back to sit on their bed, nearly enjoying the flat destination of fatigue. On her pillow lay a manila envelope with her name on it. Sam's handwriting. She opened it slowly. *I seem to touch so many people* . . . it was Sam's handwriting, but the words were from her journal, she remembered them, *touching this time of my life, pushing against people with my hands on them, moving through days and nights full of warmth* . . . a foolish vulnerable journal entry written without the protective coating of wit . . . *full of warmth touching these strangers in my life.*

There were many sheets of paper, copies of caustic letters from friends, and more in Sam's handwriting, transcriptions of her words from her journal, from letters, and from her speech, overheard, he had somehow overheard. He had taped together the pieces of a conversation with a woman in Montreal; Angela was struck how unusually articulate she'd been, how irreverent and funny, how unlike herself. *You should've been here, we tore the place up, me and Regina and even dog-face Sharon (who you'd like), no mercy, it was the nutcracker suite, we danced on the bones of every man we ever knew. God we were awful. Oh babe, Sam is home. If I go downstairs now I'll shake him up so bad he'll think he's drinking Draino. I am Not in the mood!* But there was one small piece, her own handwriting carefully pieced together and taped like a bad jigsaw, Patrick's phone number and her idle, experimental confession,

> *I find him crazy, so attractive, what's the matter with*
> *me, but I like this, it's*
> *alive.*

The phone rang and stopped in the middle of the second ring. Sam must have answered it. She left her office and walked through the dark bedroom to the landing and leaned over, listening. A creature had been let loose in the house. Downstairs it was completely quiet. She leaned over further. He was standing directly under the railing looking up at her. Startled, she said, "Wrong number?"

He paused. "He hung up."

Too many words and too long the process of selection, words like an ice jam. She moaned.

"We're getting a lot of funny calls," said Sam. Idle conversation.

She looked back to where the letters lay on their bed. A broken picture. Imagined Sam patiently taping and copying, same posture when he worked at polishing his stones, simple devotion. His dumb fingers copying. Innocent dangerous face of a sleepwalker.

Sam remained standing, looking up, something worldly, accustomed to cruelty, the betrayed husband looking at the errant wife, and within his throat an accusation or an invitation. *Confess Angela, confess, and then we will turn on every light in the house.*

Idyll

The court adjourned for the weekend, a holiday which inflicted upon Angela fatigue deep as bone marrow. For weeks she had lived in the intaglio bliss, the complete reversal of her domestic patterns, work become play, office become home. The fictitious logic of the trial had superseded real time. And her devotion to Joey had nearly eclipsed her anxiety over Sam.

On Friday night, faced with a neglected house, the laundry basket like a compost stuffed with damp towels, drawers empty of clean socks, the mirrors speckled with the synthetic spray of toothpaste, all but the liquor cabinet depleted, her exhaustion was sudden, listless as boredom. She couldn't go near him. She would imagine him going through her papers when she was out. Her desk was useless to her now. Sam's eyes kept her at bay. It was unnecessary to approach him because he was everywhere.

She took her drink to the deck and walked without shoes, tearing her stockings on the brick sidewalk that led out to the declining yard. The garden was gorgeous with purple thistle grown through the woody stems of pumpkin. Beets were the size of fists with dry red knuckles risen through the dusty top-soil. There had not yet been a frost. Green and auburn leaves, burnt orange flowers that had refused to yield fruit, ferns from carrots grown so long they were pushed back up above the earth rejected and split and greenish from sun, a garden preserved by the autumnal equinox, except for the potato plants whose over-long branches were absorbing the colours of the unturned earth, and tomatoes kneeling and bleeding. She had done this before. Angela was passionate about her garden's seeding, indif-ferent to all weeding, but its reaping was a consequence forgot-ten; by late August she was free of it and the garden was thus, at least in part, perennial; tomatoes and onions might grow again if they're not touched in autumn.

Someone far down the river was burning fall. All around her the grass was hidden under dead leaves, their ribs of chloro-phyll, black-edged with precisely circular holes like cigarette burns. Ash blue, the air. She returned to the glass ship that was Sam's house.

He was standing in the living room, his figure backlit from the last of the sun where low cloud left a long vivid line at the horizon. She was too far away to distinguish his features but Angela was certain, she and Sam were looking directly at one another. His eyes on her, sharp as a stick or a gaff, lifting her from the sea of last light. He reeled her in.

She stood beside him at the porcelain sink with her hands in her pockets, a lank posture explicit with dull fatigue. She cared only for sleep. He was washing yesterday's dishes. She knew it was a demonstration of her uselessness. She watched. When he spoke she lifted her head to him sideways, lending an ear, but her eyes remained on his hands in the soapy water and her body was stiff, struck by listening. His voice fetched her, for discipline.

"Have you got a lawyer?" he asked.

Angela was at pains to answer, her mind like Sam's pinball; his question fired off in her an overloaded response, a spinny series of contradicting trajectories. Yes she had a lawyer, she was wearing it, something like a riddle, she wondered if it would be funny and if she could tell it. He read her silence closely, attentive with all but his eyes.

"Because, baby, you're getting a divorce."

She wanted to laugh, it struck her giddy. So addicted to work had she become that now her task lay before her, to travel to the conclusion of their parallel lines, she woke to anticipation of a night's work, a seduction. She remained at Sam's side and, looking up, noticed in the vast pane of glass before her a tiny hole as from a gunshot and she put her finger on it to stop the rush of air sucking their home into shrapnel. She removed her finger and looked at it as if the pupil of glass would be embedded in her skin.

"Did someone shoot at us?"

"It was a crow, flew into the window."

She looked out the northern window and then she noticed the black figures of birds pasted everywhere, the transparent walls with a flock of shadows flown across, their intolerable shape, blackbirds, all birds, bird-shape without distinction. In her absence, Sam's house had acquired holes, real and imaginary.

From some museum inside her, she found an old phrase. "Sam I'm sorry I've been so busy."

Sam groaned. Angela resisted the slightest fracture of compassion, knowing it would be fatal for them both. She continued her reprimand. "Really Sam. I've let you go away from me before, when your business was distracting. Why can't you cut me the same slack?"

He seized her arm with his wet hand and shook her out. "You fucking cunt."

Sam's face was ancient, beyond age, seamed with wrinkles that looked like feathers, and his neck was raw from the chafing of sun and razor but his body was young. He had buttoned his shirt loosely and his chest was bare and she could see that the aging stopped beneath his throat and the rest of him would be oily smooth.

It was like a night of love. They drank and drank their midnight whisky, pouring freely and drinking from the glass with the bottle in the other hand. They had not been so intimate in years. They looked at each other from opposite ends of the house, their hostility, their broken questions and incommensurable answers eloquent with mutually unrequited love.

He said that he was tired of hearing about *a surveillance called love.* Angela recognized her own words. She felt responsible for a foolish posture but this was nothing like the repulsion she felt for his having memorized her privacy. She removed her blouse, wearing only her slip. She liked the smell of her own nervousness, curled her legs up on the couch revealing the ugly elastic crotch in her stockings, she wrapped her arms around her knees and turned her head and secretly she licked her own arm and secretly she enjoyed her own taste, the skin become dry and rough to the tongue. She accepted gracelessly as a woman on a long walk away from home the burden of her own elaborate expression, *a surveillance more intimate, a scrutiny he calls love.* Kind of a cowboy song. She wondered where he'd found it. He was a plagiarist.

It was later than it had ever been. He was standing over her running his hands over his thighs in a parody of a sexy woman, Marilyn Monroe singing her birthday song for a canny president. Sam spoke provocatively, pouting and feminine, "Is it the scent of betrayal? Will you take a bath?"

Angela hit him in the face and pulled at his mouth, scratching with pleasure his smiling lips. He enjoyed it, he seemed fulfilled. Then he took her wrists in his hands and held them to her sides. He pulled her to the floor and twisted her body over like a paisley. He put his hands on her throat and took her by her hair, the rug beneath her back, and his voice granular, an agony of sand, he said, "You want him? You want him baby?" His hand he inserted into her mouth, choking her by inserting his fingers into her throat.

The morning was simple as an empty glass. They had lain on the rug like they'd been thrown there and woke at precisely the same moment. Day. Their anger had vanished in the elliptical night leaving them stranded and shy. In the first minute of waking, she asked him if he would leave her today and he said no, his hands on her shoulders. No.

Sam and Angie spent the morning cleaning the house. When Angela carried a box of newspapers through the kitchen to the green door, she moved as if she had never walked before; Angie's motion preceded her and she tried to fill her own body. It occurred to her that Sam should apologize and bring flowers. Once, she approached him, in an exercise of self-enunciation. Sam was sitting on the floor rearranging photographs in an album. She kneeled before him. The photographs dated many years back. Angela had once fit perfectly within the dimensions of a young marriage. Thinking to touch Sam now, she took a photograph of herself from his hand, brushing his fingers. He watched her with plain expectancy. Angela looked at the photograph of herself as a simple young woman. She felt very old and large and incomplete. She touched Sam, wishing from him a gift of definition. She could see clearly then what she was not. She walked about the house, prepared for work with a body obscenely large. The noises of water, her shoes on the bare floor, the brush through her hair, the vulgar fact of her body, seeking Sam's affirmation, and failing; she had failed his expectations. She was remedial; it was too soon to say something new.

The judge in Joey's trial had suggested he would be in a position to give his verdict by early afternoon. Before she left for work she asked Sam if he would marry her. This joke was their traditional gesture of reconciliation. Sam reminded Angie that what they had was a marriage. But yes, Sam would be home when she returned. She drove downtown, her face open to all. She would maintain the precarious innocence in her own face, the childish movements, back toward the courtroom, still a little drunk, and pleased with the achievement of walking. The Crown counsel looked up quickly, saw her new posture as overconfidence.

Black-robed, she sat and waited. Around her the other lawyers and their juniors stood chatting, their faces bright with relief and the fresh rightness of formality. The courtroom had large sash windows but the room was illuminated by fluorescent squares. Their periscopic figures made triangular shadows upon the carpet.

The court was called to order. Two guards brought Joey to his seat beside Angela where they were protected from the scrutiny of the gallery by a wooden screen. They conferred quietly within this shelter.

"How do you feel?" she asked him.

"Good," he said. Because that's what she wanted him to say.

"It's going to be all right," she said.

Joey received Angela's confidence like someone listening to a refrain, to familiar and redundant patter. His hands were clasped peacefully. She'd knit him whole. And central. The judge entered. When everyone stood together, Joey smiled with pleasure. This ritual had been enacted several times a day for the past three weeks and Joey always responded well to repetition. Standing beside Angela, he was taller than she was. His chest and neck were thick from lifting weights at the Centre.

There were the scuffling of chairs and murmurs of spectators and the expelled breath of their diaphragms and coughs and then a respectful silence. Like an orchestra tuning, a beautiful sound.

The judge's face was peevish and myopic. His mouth squinted like an eye. His lungs two black speakers on either side of the bench. A vocal arrangement, larynx, electronic pulse, electric breath. Spectators welded into chrome, the colours of their summer clothing smeared by artificial light. The judge's logic, lovely as noise. The grace of logic. Elegance. What would lead a woman to learn the law? All women are taught to worship beauty. The law is beautiful because it is a mysterious and therefore effortless power. All women worship effortless power. Therefore all women worship the law. A syllogism. A headache. No such thing as all-women. The judge ordered her to consider her own failure. The defence, he said, hadn't recognized the cumulative power of each circumstantial fact. She had tried to obscure that power by distracting the court with discontinuous observations. The totality of evidence was, he said, so overwhelming, the accused must provide an explanation. But the accused is a young man who will not call himself responsible. And if he is not responsible then he is not a man worthy of our trust. He must be incarcerated until such time as he accepts responsibility. The judge did not look at Joey. He looked sternly at Angela. Joey looked at Angela too. The judge cited an authority in the Ontario Court of Appeal, 1916. Absent any explanation from the accused, he concluded, the accused is guilty as charged. The judge looked to Joey then. What he saw was proof of his own logic: a young man devoid of the grace of the law.

Angela's face was fixed in expectation of Joey's vindication, her face earnest and humble, waiting for victory. She was a self-measured opponent and could afford humility. Until now, her humour and her talent for a daughter's fidelity had made it easier for her mentors to grant those victories. Working within the system. For truth is prismatic, and this is false, and this is false. No one holds the power, not the judge, who holds it in trust as best he can. The learned judge. As best he can. He looked at her for the desperate fraction, and then resumed authority. He was very tired and he knew he had failed. A wise judge.

Her maternal body must act for Joey and though she had no presence she rose so Joey would rise when the judge left the room. The robes on a little man, a small and vicious act. She turned a smiling mouth to Joey. "He's made a mistake," she said.

"He said I did it?"

"Not exactly."

"Can I go?"

"No."

"He thinks I did it?"

"Not exactly."

He was panicking. She said, "It's going to take some time to straighten this out." The guards were coming for him. "They made a mistake. We'll fix it, don't worry, please don't worry." He was being taken away. "It's OK, Joey, don't worry. I'll fix it."

Suddenly ardent in a farce. In Joey's eyes the quick terror when the bottom falls out, and then the fast defence; he would be more ironic than his own fate. He remembered to be cool. Angela hadn't saved him. Of course not. He'd been obedient as a patient grateful for a cure, absorbed in simple concentration on his own repair. For a little while, his life had been real. He wouldn't remember the stain of her attentions, a washable tattoo. His body was deficient, the shirt too small, the running shoes too big, spine curved, bowlegged, toes in when he walks, the game's loser. Angela's. Angela's loss.

Afterwards, she stood a long time at her desk, reliving Joey's back, the curvature of his spine. Her desk was covered in paper. She could smell the paper, a dry peppery accidental odour. Over the edge of her desk, the spikes of a potted plant. Dry air, the plant in cracked soil. Carpet in points of pale yellow and green. Invisible carpet, scent of paper, her hand, edge of desk. The door to the hallway was open and she went and stood, looking. Doorways, glass, light, no shadows, no possibility, ever, of shadow.

But to say this, when the story had no longer held him in disregard, his actions had become valid and for the first time in his life Joey knew the joy of consequence. To say was to be heard and to live with an effect upon others. To live inside the breathing consonance. To be loved.

Showers

Angela left her office at dusk. The city smelled sweetly of mulch, comforting and dark. She couldn't feel the air on her skin; it had no temperature. May had apologized for the bad timing but the party for Sharon's new baby had to take place tonight because it was impossible to accommodate everyone's schedule. The timing was awful, but then babies don't pay attention to time and we will celebrate that. She imagined that it would lift her daughter's spirits to celebrate a bright new life.

The church had been alarmed and her friends had been scandalized when Sharon had baptized the baby the previous Sunday. The infant was named Mary and was swaddled in heirlooms, lacy and immense. Sharon had asked May to be godmother. The birth had given May not merely pleasure. She was unhinged from herself, a benign sacrifice of her characteristic drive, the artist's pulse which had always defined May from other mothers. The baby had completed what May's tormented hands had begun. Now when May spoke she rarely looked at her audience; her eyes were always on the baby's face as if she were seeking her own definition in the baby's fussy indifference.

May was holding the infant this way when Angela arrived. Sharon and May coddled the baby while they spoke to Angela. They asked her about the trial and expressed astonished outrage at the verdict, all the while grasping the tiny hands, kissing the tiny cheek. Their maternal solipsism evoked in Angela a hungry grief. May glanced at her, irritated: the selfless examining the self-absorbed. She ordered her daughter to have a drink and join the party. She would surely take the case to the Court of Appeal. The judge was a fool. And that boy came from such a broken place it's hard to imagine what rage he might harbour. "I know what *I'm* capable of," May said. "And I've had a lucky life." She placed the baby's head against her ruddy seamed cheeks, a gnarled setting for the opalescent infant. She closed her eyes and inhaled the baby's fragrance. Her droll voice had softened. "You're worn out," she said, and then in a singsong to the infant, "Isn't she worn out?"

"Yes," said Angela. "I must be tired, underneath." She looked at Sharon. "You have a beautiful baby."

"Thanks."

They smiled a little. Sharon shrugged, a modest collaborator.

Regina flew in. "Hello crones." She kissed them all, then looked at Angela. "Randy told me." She took Angie's arm, drew her out to the back door. "I'm phoning you tomorrow. You and I are going to talk. We're going to get you straight, my friend."

"I'm straight," said Angie.

"You're wonderful. We'll talk tomorrow."

Angela didn't think she'd feel like talking. Regina said, "I don't give a damn if you don't want to. I'm picking you up at noon. We're going out for the whole afternoon."

Angie returned to the kitchen. "I'm off." She reached up to offer Sharon a kiss.

"Appeal!" said May.

"Of course!" Chipped and bright she sang goodbye to the roomful of women. They were well dressed and stood comfortably on expensive shoes speaking of business and the health of their parents. Angela placed her hands in the silk pockets of her jacket. "The enemy is always stupid." The company laughed as they would have laughed at anything she said just then; such was the timing for laughter and wit.

Sharon stopped her at the door. "Tough day dear," Sharon said. She put her arms around Angela, squeezed, and then put her palm on her face. "Tough break. Just get on with the appeal. You'll feel better."

"Sure."

"Did you do the splatter guy?"

"No."

Sharon let go, permitting only the quickest appraisal; it would be impolite to judge.

"I didn't get him." Angela was wandering toward confession.

"Well. These things happen."

"I didn't think I'd need him."

"It's expensive, yeah, bringing these guys in. And anyway, you're right. Any idiot could have a look at the pictures and wonder where all that blood went when it didn't go on Joey."

"It did seem kind of self-evident. Joey was pretty clean."

"Absolutely. Just a mistake. The judge blew it."

"Well." Angela plucked at the corsage on Sharon's dress. Sharon had refined the style of her maternity, but still she was soft and draped in rich colour. There was a spaciousness in her demeanour, home from travel, the streets smaller and easily navigated. Sharon's irises looked like chamois, brushed filaments of brown with gold flecks like the sun got in them.

"You're really wrung out," Sharon said. Angie had started to cry. Sharon hid her from the party and took her back to the kitchen where May sat at the table nuzzling the baby. They were sober, the two mothers. "Sam has been reading my mail," Angela said. They waited for the real information. "I guess it surprised me."

"Your father used to read mine," said May. To Sharon, "He was completely blatant about it. I didn't give a damn. There wasn't anything there he didn't already know." She looked with mild curiosity at her daughter.

Angela smiled a little. "I'm fried," she said.

Angela drove home feeling late. Sam's house seemed to her like
a crucial oversight. It looked utterly finished, as if it had gone
on without her. Parked beside Sam's car was a shiny old
Mustang, as cool as Jimmy Dean. She hurried into the house
with a lurching obsequious craving.

She heard their voices and knew it was Patrick that Sam
spoke to before she saw their heads over the top of the couch,
looking vulnerable and disembodied. Their boyish complicity
was at odds with Sam's talent for temporization, his stillness,
his watchful inertia. Patrick was wearing a bleached linen shirt
over a white undershirt, and a small silver earring. He had a
hybrid sort of integrity. Angela realized that she liked him for
this. He was truly and ingeniously beyond pain or difficulty. He
played lightly on the surface because he rejected its super-
structure. He'd changed his hair, wore it messed up with a two-
day beard. They said hello and Sam asked about the verdict.
Sam listened with his head at an angle. Patrick listened with
infinite patience.

Sam stood up to greet her, the serene lines of his long legs,
his long waist, tall, impeccable, his eyes narrow. It was quite
dark. She brought with her a yellow light that stayed within the
spools of her hair, her pink coat and a familiar scent of
maraschino. She walked in like a painting of a woman, like an
idea of a woman. Like a cut in Sam's white skin.

"We lost," she told them.

Patrick half-turned, his movements graceful. He raised his
eyebrows and made a sympathetic noise expressing faint surprise. He crossed his legs. Angela, looking at him, liked him
immensely, a friend despite all. His limitations a given. She
thought with a wild hope, he was their first mutual friend in a
long time. The room was suddenly warped as a frozen river, she
thought she could hear ice moan, that whale song river-ice will
make. There was a CD playing jazz with a muted trumpet.

She looked at her husband. "We lost," she said again, this
time beseeching.

Sam spoke gently, quizzical. "You're not that surprised are you Angie?"

"Yes! Well I thought, yes! I thought it was obvious. You saw Joey. He's, he's. I was so sure."

Sam nearly went to her then. He put his hands behind him and chewed something with his front teeth.

"I was too sure," Angela said. "I thought. I was too sure. I thought I was working so hard. I was looking in the wrong places." She looked shiny and untouchable like she'd been brushed with egg-white. Her words of despair were spoken in her lush mezzo.

Patrick said, "You're always so tough on yourself, Angie." Sam looked at him. "She really is," Patrick said. "All the time." The jazz was painful, its distortions grinding against their speech.

"It's dark in here!" she scolded like a wife returning with her benefactions of repetition and warmth. She turned on the big kitchen light which they never used and it changed the room into a public place, a waiting room. They looked at one another and saw they were older and worn.

The three of them seemed to move like birds, spasmodic, at a tilt. Patrick seated, Angela standing where she'd come in. Sam stood sadly speculative. He gestured to Angela as if they were alone in the house. His hands indicated Patrick, Exhibit A. He lifted his shoulders, to say, It's obvious, stop running. Between us, everything is fully lit. Sam's vision was exact; it saw the blue bones beneath her soft motion. The body outruns our wishes.

His secret preceded everything. It made all else betrayal. Sam knew the true significance of Angela's smile, Patrick's slow-blinking calm. And he marked it. And because day had shifted into night and Angela walked past and Patrick enjoyed his drink, and friendships formed and failed, and strangers know her name, the world was an encyclopedia of betrayal. Angela could make herself as fine as a line for him, as small as a sip. But Sam knew she was in excess, she was colouring outside the lines. She was getting that stiff mouth she gets when she knows she's been outplayed.

Angela's spine was singed by fear, like paper curled in fire. The bebop jazz, a heart without sentiment. She would join the resistance. She travelled the idle warp in the carpet, across the room she performed a mannequin's walk toward Patrick and madly offered to shake his hand, looking at Sam, Exhibit B. Friendship. Then she stood with her high heels on tiptoe and kissed her husband's cheek and she lifted her left toe behind her. Sam was cool, cool as stone.

She took his hand and pulled him to the kitchen. It was Blondie talking to Dagwood but it would have to do till the dry body would lose some territory to hope. A parody of health being better than none at all. She marched him like a newlywed to a corner of the glass room where the jazz served as wall, as aural if not visual border.

"You must be shook up," Sam said, expectant.

She nodded. She touched his neck. He pulled away. She said she loved him. He nodded. She said again, "I do love you Sam."

Very calm, tenderly, Sam said, "Why don't you shut up."

He looked at Patrick.

"It's funny you'd make friends with him," said Angie. "I wanted you to. He's nice isn't he? Not a giant mind, but he is what he is."

Sam dropped his shoulders and his head backward in a lonely gesture of despair.

She said, "Now that the trial's over, maybe we could go away for a few days. That's awful of me, isn't it? Joey's still in jail." Her voice evaporated. She saw that Joey had made a big space in her, that it would not go away. "I'm exhausted. Will you come to bed? Send Patrick home and come to bed." She wasn't convincing. Sam was a stranger; it would be like adultery to touch him now. She knew that she would never do that again.

"You want another drink, Patrick?" asked Sam.

Patrick looked at his gin and tonic. Shrugged. "Sure," he said.

Angela stopped to say good night to Patrick. He was a well-wisher at a train station, standing on the platform while the train had already started to move, and she was leaving him behind, waving through the window, pressing her face against the glass. She climbed the stairs, still wearing pink high heels, her stockings brushing and whispering. Everywhere the broken bubbles of their distant conversation. Patrick laughed. Sam was telling a story; she could hear his animation but not the words. Angela's portion of the house was very small, it had nearly disappeared.

His copies were still scattered on the floor. Angela read them many times. She read very carefully the seams where they'd been taped together. Her words were familiar, candid, more fully and intimately hers now that he'd taken them. His entry had returned them to her like a brand on her own tongue.

She lay down fully dressed, listening for their voices. When she shut her eyes, the place where her body fell through the air was the centre of an onion. She fell through the centre and then when the falling grew so tight it closed on her it threw her into the air and that is where she stayed. Looking at Sam's house through the glass, from the other side. She had nowhere to go but to sleep. So she slept.

Night when she woke. The house dark. Blank silence, electrical, static sounds. The house seemed empty. She felt her way downstairs. The green door was open. Sweet smell of grass burning, and the nearness of rain. Outside she could hear someone digging, a shovel in soil. She walked to her garden. She saw Sam's white shirt, his motion, the wheelbarrow beside him. He was digging up the garden, his spade cutting the plants, turning them under. He threw the stalks into the fire. The large roots, the remaining tubers, he lifted and shook and deposited into the wheelbarrow. He was preparing the garden for winter. It was mild with a summerlike breeze and winter seemed endlessly postponed. The shadows were green. Sam knew she was there. His action grew more determined but he didn't acknowledge her. She stood several feet away.

"Are you coming up?" She could say this without the inflection of hope.

Sam nodded. She returned to the house. She went to their bedroom, removed her clothes and lay beneath the sheets in the cool comfort of bed. Sam appeared. He sat down, moving her leg out of the way. And so began their second night of love. He raised his hand and began to strike her, a lyrical contact, legs or face or torso, unplanned contact, here and there. He clasped his hands and raised his arms and brought them down on her. Many times, arms above his head, hands together, and down. His sounds were the sounds he'd made digging and carried with them the same force of serious work and intention. Angela might have screamed or groaned, she might have been laughing. He was alert to sounds beyond her hearing. He carried out his attack as if she were silent, as if it were light. His ears were filled with the roaring of his own wings.

When Angela was still, Sam left her there and walked about his house. He covered the entire house with the silence of his flight. As he walked, he gathered his polished stones in his pockets, filling himself with their cool shine. Sam stood in his glass house looking out. He took the smallest stone from his pocket. He put it under his tongue. Then he quietly returned to his garden.

Angie lay still, timing his passage, from the loft and down, through the kitchen and out, where the grass fire would smoulder slowly. She sat up like a sick child, feeling her bruises. The pain was a guide. She dressed. She walked downstairs and left by the front door. Every muscle had fisted. Every step strangely violated the pain. She imagined Sam's eyes on her back, and stood straight while she walked down the long driveway between the maple trees. She would soon be out of sight. When she reached the gate, she slipped under, grunting when the pain knuckled her, every bone and muscle. Then she went along the boulevard. She was moaning something with each breath, a low kind of chant undulating. Her feet were bare, the grass wet and cool and surprising. Broad puddles spilled by the side of the road, full of inky rippling light, and she went to one and stepped down off the curb into a couple of inches of water, warm as blood, warm the way a lake is warm in the rain.

A car approached. She hurried from the road and hid behind the trees and waited while it passed. Red lights reflected on the black pavement. Before he was out of sight, he stopped. His car remained idling at the side of the road, brake lights like a beacon, and the patient mumbling engine.

The road followed a broad slow curve. On either side, tall stands of ash trees, Russian olive, and some elm, black branches, a wide green boulevard cleared of fallen leaves. Behind the trees, a low fence. She climbed the fence. Then she was in the dark, lit by a pink sky. She could walk away from the road. Sam couldn't see her now. There was a thread between them, bright as mercury. But broken. Severed cleanly. She could feel that, too.

Behind her, the night closed, clear, simple, empty. This would be solitude. An unseasonal night. Very wet. It must have been raining for a long time. This was not possible. But then it was true. Very lightly.